Escape to Valencia Cove

# JULIET BRILEE

# CHRISTMAS
## Cake Day

# ACKNOWLEDGMENTS

I'd like to thank Susie, Dineen, and Larry for their help. I also extend gratitude to Jill, Gail, and Diane, the cake baking wonder women, who introduced me to family favorites: candy cane cake, and coconut cake made with freshly ground coconuts. I also thank Josh, who is totally blind, for his ongoing insights about navigating a sighted world when one is visually impaired.

# 1

Olivia Brighton pulled off the interstate in Pensacola, rubbed her scalp with her fingertips and groaned. Dallas was another ten hours. What was she thinking? She sped onto the highway in the opposite direction and, at the first rest area, called her cousin to make sure it was okay to come. Anna's friendly voice sealed it. For the rest of the day she dodged holiday traffic and winter residents driving south. A south Florida Christmas hadn't been on her radar for the holidays this year. Neither had being divorced.

It was nearly midnight when the Valencia Cove exit came into view. She blinked heavy lids, rolled her shoulders, pulled down the exit ramp and ran over something hard. Her heart jumped. *Whoa!* That woke her up. Gripping the steering wheel with tight hands, she swerved around glass and metal debris covering the road. She pulled onto Palmetto Drive, released the breath she'd been holding and flexed her fingers.

The humidity would frizz her wavy hair. She lowered the window anyway. Tropical air that smelled like home rushed in and she smiled. The small, coastal town where she'd grown up would make a good place to regroup and launch Olivia 2.0.

Houses along the quiet, dark road sat tucked between orange groves and pine flatwoods. Only the big moon hovering at the horizon lit the landscape. She pulled up her holiday playlist and hummed along with "Silent Night."

The car bumped across the old railroad tracks and got a short distance. Thump, thump, whomp. *What's that?* On full alert, she bolted upright, her forehead pulling tight as she eased the RAV4 to a stop. After a day of driving, standing on her bad ankle could be a problem. She stood carefully and hobbled around to check the tire. *Oh, for crying out loud. A flat.* Thank goodness she had roadside service with the auto club. A quick call and the representative said a truck would arrive within ninety minutes.

She drummed her fingers on the steering wheel and peered into the night. *It's so dark.* Unnerving. Anna and Mark could help, but she hated to wake them, and how independent would she look if their assistance was required before she'd even gotten to their house? What if she fixed it herself? She opened the back to retrieve the spare tire and a jack from the cargo hold. *Darn it!* Several heavy items would need to be moved to get to the spare. She blew out an aggravated breath and stacked her suitcases and bins on the shoulder of the road.

Thank goodness for the flashlight on her phone. She scrutinized the tire stored in the cargo area. The spare for her old Civic had been heavy, but this one was ridiculous. Perhaps she ought to wait. Headlights briefly shone on her bins as a vehicle sped by in the other direction. Then black night swallowed the scene.

About a quarter mile down, the vehicle that had passed her turned around. It rolled to a stop on the shoulder about twenty feet back and cut the headlights.

The auto club was sending a truck. This couldn't be them.

Anxiety coiled in her chest as she registered a large man hop out and crunch the gravel shoulder, coming her way. She backed up a step and grabbed the lug wrench, a makeshift weapon. There was no running—her ankle was still weak, and she couldn't drive on the flat tire and leave all her boxes. Feeling like a sitting duck, she strengthened her grip on the hard, cold metal of the wrench and tightened her arm.

"Need a hand?" It was too dark to see his features clearly.

"I've got this." Damsel-in-distress wasn't her style. "Looks like I have a flat. I was getting out the jack and spare." She swung the wrench back and forth in case he got any ideas.

"You sure I can't give you a hand? Those spares can be difficult to manage." He stayed put.

Probably didn't want to get within range of her weapon.

"Well. Okay... since you took the time to stop."

Did he chuckle? "Kind of you to allow me." He lifted out the spare like it was nothing and grabbed her jack. "May I?" He held out his palm.

She handed over the lug wrench, and he made quick work of the change. From a few feet away, she cataloged his jeans and boots and a dark tee shirt. It might come in handy if she needed to identify him later. But if he was going to mug her, the man probably wouldn't fix her tire first. She released a long and hard breath. *I must be delirious from the drive.*

When he began tightening the lug nuts, he finally spoke. "I noticed you limping. Why don't you get off your feet? I'll load her back up."

"I can't allow you—"

"It's Christmas. Let me do this."

She climbed in the driver's seat and locked her door for good measure.

A few minutes later he announced, "All set," tapped the roof of her vehicle, and walked into the night.

She called out, "Thank you," a waste of breath, since he was back to his Jeep. Only after she pulled back onto the road did she realize she'd never gotten his name. And now she was late.

≋≋≋

Were her cousins asleep? Almost one a.m., their house was still sparkling with Christmas lights and brightly lit reindeer decorations. Olivia sat in the driveway, basking in the glow, her body still vibrating with nerves from the long trip. A full day with her foot on the gas probably wasn't what her doctor had in mind when he'd told her she could begin driving again. She cautiously stepped out of her car.

The front door swung open. Anna must've been waiting by the window. "You're here." Her cousin met her halfway and enfolded her in a cinnamon-scented hug.

Mark followed Anna, looking like he'd just woken up. He gave her a squeeze and used his old name for her. "Hey, Livy Belle." He raised his eyebrows. "Got the kitchen sink in there?" He pried her two large suitcases from among the boxes and totes crammed tightly into the car. Yes, she was moving. Where, she didn't know. She'd left that part out when she'd called. Even though her old roommate said she could come to Ft. Myers, she'd probably wind up moving to Dallas with her mother. Thirty-four was too old to be a boomerang kid and live with Mom, but her options were limited. For now, she'd give herself the gift of a holiday with the people who felt most like home to her, Anna and Mark Hastings.

~~~~~

Olivia sunk her five-foot-seven frame into Anna's sofa and relaxed, breathing in the fragrance of the twinkling Douglas fir. It had to be a natural antidepressant. Steele was allergic to Christmas trees, and she'd forgotten how much she loved the scent.

"A good Samaritan stopped and helped you with the flat? You could have called us. Mark would've come." Anna appeared mildly alarmed.

"I know. I didn't want to bother him, but I could use his help to get it repaired." She surveyed the room, fully decked out with a manger scene, little Santa figurines, angels, and greenery, a testament to her cousin's domestic talents. "You could go pro on holiday decorating. I feel like I've landed on the cover of a Christmas magazine."

Anna smiled at the compliment. "Let me get you something to eat."

A gray tabby jumped to the couch. He rubbed his face on her arm, purring. "You still have Tiger. What is he, close to fifteen now?"

"And bad as ever. So watch out, he still scratches." Her cousin offered her a sandwich and a plate loaded with a variety of frosted Christmas cookies. "It's so good to have you here." Anna's short dark hair was touched with silver, her cardigan fit more snugly, and she was still the best nurturer Olivia knew.

She tried a cookie. "These are so good. Now I know why you smell like cinnamon."

"I was trying out a new recipe." Anna shrugged. "How was the drive? And what a treat to have you here for cake-baking day this year."

Olivia paused mid-bite, anxiety making it difficult to swallow. "Cake-baking day?" She kept her voice positive. "That's right. Is everyone still coming over for that?" How had she forgotten? It was almost a holiday of its own and more work than most.

"You don't sound excited." Anna narrowed her eyes. "You always loved baking Christmas cakes."

"I do, but lately I've felt like a vampire got to me and sucked me dry."

"You've been through a lot. It might lift your spirits."

She groaned. Was it wise to be at Anna's house where everyone would buzz with holiday cheer? The thought of hunkering down alone, watching Christmas movies and eating microwaved turkey dinner was starting to seem like the better alternative.

"Did you ever find a job?" Anna waited, her expression maternal, patient.

"No. There's been a hiring freeze. Before I broke my ankle, I was substitute teaching. Then I got hurt. It's been challenging." She gathered a breath past her frustration and let out a long sigh. "I'm glad I found the nerve to call and ask to come for Christmas. Thank you."

Anna waved. "Don't be silly. We enjoy having you. And we want you to stay through to celebrate New Year's Day."

"I'd love to." Now she had extra time to work up to asking her mother if she could move in. Anna and Mark had done enough for her. Five years earlier, Anna had lost her mom. Then their daughter, Stephanie, had died in a car accident. She didn't want to be a burden to her cousins.

"You want to talk or go to bed? I doubt those dark circles are from the drive."

"It's been a tough fall. Aside from trying to find work, getting divorced, and..." She waved at her foot and grimaced.

Anna nodded. "Tara said something about how much trouble you've been having."

She snapped to attention. "Ah, yes, the family telegraph." What had Tara said? She was supposed to be keeping everything confidential. "As you can see, I've been stress eating."

"No, the extra weight looks good on you."

Olivia glanced toward the ceiling and shook her head. "You don't have to say that." She paused, working out the short version. "I didn't get hired for any of the jobs I applied for, and Steele took that big portrait job last May, which was the beginning of the end."

"How so? It wasn't unusual for him to travel, was it? Did he quit his job at the university?"

"No, he still taught during the week. He traveled for commissions on the weekends." She groaned. That was the problem with marrying a talented portrait artist. "He returned to that May commission at the end of September and when he got home, I found a photo... an ultrasound." It still made her feel like she'd eaten ground glass when she thought about that day.

"No! Was it...?"

She nodded, the hurt coming back all over again. "The girl was pregnant from when he was there Memorial Day. He wasn't going to cut it off. It wasn't the first time he'd been unfaithful. But." She paused. The ugly scene replayed through her mind. "I stormed out, tripped in the parking lot and broke my ankle. Great getaway, huh?" They sat in silence for a long moment.

She rubbed circles across her forehead as though she could push the memories from her head.

"I'm sorry, honey. Time will help." Anna squeezed her arm. "Let me show you to your room. I converted the grey room to the sewing room. The girls are staying in the room next to mine."

Mark had already put her bags in the blue guest room. She rooted around her smaller suitcase for aspirin and chocolate. As the candy melted in her mouth, she surveyed the photos on the wall. "When did you take these?" There was her cousin Blessie, brushing an adorable miniature horse with some nice-looking guy who was partly cut off. In another photograph she was holding a ribbon and a basket of strawberries beside the same handsome man.

"That's over at Sacred Haven Center. She loves it there. And that one's from the county fair. Her teacher helped her enter."

"Who's that guy with Blessie?" It nagged at her. He seemed familiar.

Anna wandered closer. "Oh." She chuckled. "That's her teacher, Trevor. He's really good with the folks at Sacred Haven. He is rather easy on the eyes."

She chewed her bottom lip. The man was nice-looking and wasn't wearing a wedding ring, but she wasn't staying in town, so why did it matter? Her life was completely up in the air.

"**O**uch." Bang. Whining.

Olivia woke up to arguing.

"No, that's my hair tie. Give it back, Pixie." The girls were up and feisty as ever.

She stretched an arm across Anna's soft homemade quilt and cracked open her lids. It'd been months since she'd slept so deeply. A powder-blue sky greeted her through palm fronds crisscrossing the window. What's that wonderful aroma? Banana? Toasted pecans? Pans clanging and the whir of the mixer sounded from the other end of the house. Was Anna already making the cakes?

Soon the house would fill with her cousins and second cousins working like the elves in Santa's workshop, cranking out one Christmas cake after another. *So much holiday cheer.* Could she get into the holiday spirit this year and face the big baking event with her emotions still raw?

Anna poked her head in the door. "Hey, Olivia, you up? I've made a fresh pot of Jake's holiday blend."

"Yes. I'm up." Like she had a choice with the girls in the next room. She rotated her foot, still recovering, wanting to be careful so she could get back to working. Steele had given her a few checks, but the money was nearly gone. She could ask her Mom and step-father for help, but it'd be a trade. Money meant control to Lydia, and Olivia hated giving her mother that power.

She checked her phone. The first from Mom. *Let's talk on Christmas Day.*

No surprise there. She and Phillip typically had a Christmas Eve party at their country club. If she wanted a home-style holiday, driving south to Anna and Mark's made the most sense.

The next text was from Maria. *Checking in. Remember—you're better off without him. Do your yoga and don't forget about the book.*

*Ha. The book.* She'd already forgotten. It'd been a going-away present. *A No-Limits Holiday.* She'd set it aside, but it was in that suitcase somewhere. She dug around, found it, and opened to a random page. *"Take time for self-care and give from a place of fullness."* Covered. Several weeks ago, Maria had driven her to a chair yoga class in the basement of St. Anthony's. The music and stretching had turned her attitude around. After that, she'd found a chair yoga class on television. Could she continue it here?

On the next page, it said, *"Focus on the positive."* Ugh. She'd become an expert at finding things to grumble about. Hadn't getting divorced, injured, and losing her job given her the right to be bitchy? Maybe it did. But if she was going to live among other humans, she ought to make a better effort. Today, she'd find things to appreciate.

Tiger slipped into the door and wove himself around her feet, purring. Okay, she'd appreciate the cat. She reached down to pet him. He whipped his head around and gave her a little swat. "You're bad." He jumped up and purred. *Yep, same old Tiger.*

The mouth-watering scent of baking drifted in from the kitchen. Now that was something she could really appreciate. She squeezed into her leggings, tighter than she'd remembered, slipped into her hip-hiding chambray shirt, and pulled on the ankle brace. Ready or not, once she showed her face, she'd be swept up in the tide of baking.

Trevor Weston pulled off his work gloves and wiped his forehead on a faded blue shirtsleeve. Over the past couple of hours, he and his students had harvested greens and tended strawberries. More plants would be set out after the chance of frost passed.

The squeal of power tools pulled his attention to the construction site that had claimed the land between the road and Sacred Haven Center for People with Disabilities. The outdoor programs manager surveyed the stretch from the garden to where palm trees lined the access road, frowned, and ground the enamel off his molars. The developer had approached the Center, wanting to acquire that chunk of land and more. How would he stop it? Everything that mattered to him was on the line.

Across the grounds, his assistant and a volunteer guided children around the ring atop the sweet Palomino and the old bay, Sandy. The developer wasn't asking for the area by the stable. But if he lost his job, the therapeutic riding program would likely end too.

"Mr. Weston." Blessie broke into his thoughts. "Can I have Tommy's part since he's gone now?" Short and chubby with brown eyes, silky cocoa hair, and an easy laugh, she turned in his direction. "Please? We can plant more strawberries there."

*Will the garden even be here when the berries ripen?* The students would be upset and lose a valuable opportunity if the garden program were to be cut. He wrestled with his response, not wanting to upset her prematurely.

Blessie pushed her hair out of her face and got a smudge of dirt on her forehead. "Pretty soon we're gonna have so many berries. Strawberry shortcake, strawberry pie, strawberries for breakfast..."

"Yes, I get the idea." He laughed softly. "Let's plant that section together. We can plant nasturtiums along the border. It'll be real pretty." *If the sale doesn't go through and we still have a garden.* "Okay, everyone. Time to put away the tools and get cleaned up."

Three of the students put their tools in the shed and walked toward the building. Blessie didn't budge. "I don't wanna go." She shot him a frown, stuck out her tongue, and concentrated on her patch of earth. Each resident had their assigned area. She loved the garden as much as he did.

"Five more minutes. That's all." He pulled on his gloves, knelt beside her, and worked for a few minutes.

After a while he stood, brushed dirt from his jeans, and exhaled hard, exhausted. Last night he'd run out late to pick up coffee and antacids. On the way back, he'd stopped to change someone's flat. When he'd returned, he'd been all wound up and had walked the grounds until two. Even though he'd enjoyed helping that woman, it'd cost him sleep.

"Let's go in now. Snack time's about to start, and someone will be here pretty soon to pick you up."

"That's right, Mr. Weston. Today's cake day. Cake day! Chocolate frosting. Coconut cake. Candy cane cake. Do you know what, Mr. Weston? Christmas is my favorite holiday. And you know what? Anna told me Olivia will be here too. She's an art teacher. She's a real artist. Olivia will help make the Christmas cakes." Blessie hummed "Jingle Bells" as they put the garden tools away.

He raked a hand through his hair and surveyed the area, making sure the tools were all collected. Out here, where the air carried the scent of pine and flowers, with horses and the garden, he found peace. Until Seaside Development ripped out the woods and filled in the wetland. His gut twisted. They'd scuttled the foxes and hawks that had called the neighboring piece of wild Florida home. If the sale goes through, this could be his last season.

Trevor walked Blessie to the main building and ducked into the office to collect his mail.

"Did you see the memo?" Jeanette Bridges, the academic programs administrator, cut him a grim glance.

He unfolded the paper at the top of his stack and groaned. "They've moved the closing on the property up to the end of next week?" Dread churned in his gut. "How can they do that? It's the week between Christmas and New Year's Day? People are out of town or busy with the holidays."

"That's probably what they're counting on." Her gaze softened. "I'm sorry. Let me know if there's anything I can do. I already submitted a letter to the board. You know you have my full support."

"Thanks, Jeanette. Good to know I have allies." Lip curling, he regarded the memo as though it were filth, acid rising in his throat. Now he had to work even faster to save his programs from the budget axe. And not only for the students. The folks at Sacred Haven Center were like his family.

Trevor muttered a few words he'd never say around his students and headed around back to where he and the groundskeeper, Edgar, had cottages. While he walked, he glanced at his mail. A bunch of ads and a card from his sister. His heart sunk. Why'd he keep hoping he'd get a response, anything, from his daughter?

He opened the door to his tan stucco cottage, and his scruffy terrier greeted him with enthusiastic yips. "Okay, Molly. Settle down." He popped an antacid, leashed the dog, and took her out to walk the fence and check the rose garden he'd planted last spring. Cooler now, the roses were in their glory, bigger and sweeter smelling. Accomplishment lifted his chest with pride. Scarlet blossoms covered the Veteran's Honor and Mr. Lincoln bushes. Yellow-green flowers covered the St. Patrick. He made a mental note to pick roses and arrange them for the program.

In another life, he'd have a sweetheart to present with a bouquet. Now he lived like a monk. For a moment, his chest ached. He fought it back. It'd been years, but Stacy's indiscretions had soured him. He'd age as a bachelor. That was how he wanted it.

"You're my buddy, aren't you, Molly?" He scratched the terrier mix. The center took all his energy and then some, with no time to waste looking for a woman who'd only be trouble in the long run. Now his mission had to be making sure the programs he'd built didn't get gutted.

his was the day Anna loved the most, the day before Christmas Eve. Cake day. She puttered in the quiet morning, humming carols with her first cup of coffee, inhaling the fragrance of ripe bananas peeled for the Bundt cake. Today, she and her cousins would bake cakes for the annual Christmas Eve gathering and make additional cakes and cupcakes to donate.

With a satisfied smile, she admired the decorations that brightened every corner of her immaculate kitchen. There were reindeer candlestick holders, holly garland, Christmas linens, and her favorite, a ceramic Christmas tree her mom had made.

Her granddaughters, Emily and Pixie, bounded into the kitchen.

"Can I lick the bowl?" Emily reached up.

"No, I want the spoon." Pixie moved in front of her older sister.

"Ouch. She pinched me." Emily rubbed her arm and glared at her little sister.

"Try to get along. It's Christmas. And this cake is banana. You like the vanilla." Anna continued mashing the bananas.

"Simmer down, girls. Find your shoes." Mark herded them from the kitchen. She smiled at her gentle giant of a husband, so good with his little granddaughters. Eight years her senior, he'd played college football until a knee injury had sent him on a tech path and he was now a semi-retired computer geek. "Hey, sugar, we're leaving shortly." He nuzzled her neck.

She turned for a quick kiss, then folded bananas into the batter and filled the Bundt pan.

Mark swiped the bowl with a finger. "Mm, banana cake, my favorite."

She stood at the oven and sighed long and hard, a feeling of heaviness immobilizing her.

"You okay, sweetheart?" He turned her around and kissed her forehead.

"Thinking about Steph." This was the fifth Christmas without their daughter, who'd died, leaving behind the two girls and their son-in-law, Brent. Pixie had been a newborn and Emily in preschool when they'd buried Stephanie.

"I know." He put his chin on top of her head and hugged her. "Me too."

"And the girls. With Brent marrying Rena... She's kind to them, but I feel like we're losing Brent, and maybe the girls too."

"I'm sure he'll still let the girls come visit." He squeezed her, then stepped back. "What time are your aunt and uncle getting in?"

"Tomorrow afternoon, late." She sniffed. "They were supposed to sit with us at the holiday program, but now they'll miss it entirely."

He softened his voice and used his *delivering bad news* tone. "Matthew texted. He and Natalie probably won't get to town until after Blessie's program tomorrow. So, I guess Lindsay will only get a few hours to play with Emily and Pixie."

She cast him a sharp look. "Brent said the girls could stay overnight."

"Brent texted too." Mark seemed to be bracing himself for her reaction. "He's picking the girls up tomorrow night at seven. They're heading to Jacksonville early."

"Oh, darn, it's so rare to have all the girls together." Her chest fell with disappointment. "At least Santa Claus will come here this year for Lindsay. I guess everyone will make it when they make it." She tried to put cheer in her voice, but this holiday was falling apart.

The girls roared back into the kitchen. "Do we get to ride in the new truck, Grandpa?" Emily jumped up and down in her new cowgirl boots. "And we'll get to see the horses?"

"Yes, we're taking the new truck. And you might get to see horses when we get Blessie. That's a maybe."

A couple of months ago, Mark bought the truck and was pressuring her to retire when the school year ended so they could pull a RV and tour the country. Nice dream, but how could they make that work? She needed to be on hand for Blessie. Even though her sister lived at Sacred Haven, she was still a part of their lives.

"Hug." Pixie stretched her arms up. "Will we get to bake the candy cane cake, Grandma?"

"Yes. When you come back. What's that in your sticky hand? Are you already eating candy canes?" The girls had been with them since school had gotten out for the holiday. Anna kissed Pixie's cheek—she smelled so good. Baby shampoo, candy canes... and, had she gotten into her perfume again?

"Pixie, you can't wear those play high heels to the park. Go find your shoes." Mark shooed them out of the kitchen for the second time.

She watched the girls go, a sinking feeling in her belly. When they moved to Jacksonville with their dad and Rena, would she and Mark still fit into their lives?

The girls' giggles and shrieks got louder.

"Quiet down, girls," Mark loud whispered from the door of the kitchen. He turned back to her. "How can Olivia sleep through that?" He shook his head and the side of his mouth edged up. "It's nice having her here without Steele."

She returned a guilty grin. "True. I always had an uncomfortable feeling around him. Tara implied he's the reason Olivia stayed away at Christmas all these years."

"Don't you think Livy looked... really tired and stressed?" Mark's gaze darkened. "And her car's packed to the gills, like she has everything she owns crammed in there. She even brought her sewing machines. Is she moving?"

≈≈≈

Olivia put on a happy face and surveyed the kitchen for things to appreciate. She found Anna at the sink. "It smells so good. Banana cake?"

"Yes, I just put it in. One made and one in the oven and..." she gestured with a soapy hand, "...a fresh pot of coffee. I'm so glad you came down this Christmas. Help yourself to fruit or those biscuits."

She poured her coffee and gazed longingly at the sugar bowl. Okay, one spoon. Two was better, three was perfect, but getting a grip on her sweet tooth needed to happen. She sipped the spicy-holiday-flavored coffee and carried it to the table. The bitter brew did nothing for the hollow feeling... in her chest.

"What have you heard from your mom?"

"Got a text. I need to talk to her. She'll spend Christmas Day with Connor as usual."

"I'm sure your brother wants her there for his girls."

"Probably. I can't compete with him and the kids. We never went out there. Steele preferred to meet up with his friends for holidays." She winced. It sounded better than it was.

"We got lucky. You're with us." Anna dried her hands and stood next to her at the window.

"Aw, thanks." She smiled at her cousin and angled her head toward the yard. "Look at all them." A flock of white ibis poked long beaks into the grass between the house and the creek. Down on the dock, two blue herons eyed the area. One flapped to the brackish water, darted his head downward, and came up with a fish. "I forgot how many birds you get here on the creek."

"I love watching the cardinals at the feeder and I put up a hummingbird feeder. Sometimes we get a few in the winter. They like that Mexican sage."

"And the decorations you've tucked around the kitchen are really nice." Bringing her attention to pleasant things did help her mood, but it didn't make her coffee any sweeter.

"Thank you. I'm going to help Mark get the girls in the car. You'll be okay out here?" Anna glanced at the brace on her foot.

"Don't worry, you don't need to wait on me. If I'm on my foot a lot, it aches. It's better now." Until she'd driven all day. Now it throbbed. She used the ultrasound machine for bone-healing daily. Why wasn't it healed by now?

"Olivia! You're here." Pixie and Emily tore into the kitchen and hugged her at the same time.

"Hey, don't knock me over." She balanced her cup to keep from spilling coffee and gave her cousins a one-armed hug. Their happy energy contagious, she broke into a wide grin.

"Come on, girls, Grandpa's ready to go." Anna led them to the front door

A moment later, voices at the side of the house warned her to get ready. The door from the garage flew open, and two cousins breezed in.

## 4

*O*livia braced her brain for the chaos of having her extended family descend on the kitchen. Cousins, second cousins, the people she'd grown up with, gathered regularly and made a point to come for Christmas cake baking day. After spending so much time alone over the past couple of months, this would feel like a circus and required another cup of coffee.

Madison lugged in a large tote. "Stand back—this thing weighs a ton." She deposited the heavy tote in front of the counter and began unloading.

"You made it." Lexie's bubbly energy lit up her face. She dropped her bag and darted over for a hug. "We're together for cake day this year. Can you believe it?"

Olivia smiled broadly at her cousin, who'd been like an older sister growing up. "Right? It's been so long."

"Too long." Lexie gave her the once-over and lowered her brows, disapproving. "You're pale. Have you been sleeping okay? You really need a beach vacation—just sayin'." She pulled her in for another squeeze and said softly, "It's so good to see you, girl."

"You look great and stayed so trim. I've..."

Lexie held up a hand. "You're voluptuous. You needed to gain weight."

"It's common for people to gain weight when they're sitting around recovering from an injury," Madison deadpanned. "You can go on a low-carb diet, and it'll probably melt off." An administrator in the hospital education department, Encyclopedia Maddipedia might not mean to be a know-it-all, but she rarely held back.

"Low-carb? Like that's gonna happen." Olivia huffed. She'd packed an extra-large bag of chocolate.

Madison surveyed the kitchen, brows drawing together. "Where's Anna? Don't tell me there's already a cake in the oven? You guys started without us? Why does she do that?"

"Don't look at me. I just got up. I haven't done a thing yet." Olivia sat back down. "Anna's helping Mark get the girls in the car."

"Madison, baking's her therapy." Lexie cast her niece a sidelong glance. "My guess is, she can't resist a head start. Don't take it personally."

"Are you two still roommates?" Olivia held back a knowing smile. It couldn't be easy living with Madison, even though she had a good heart.

"Yes, since Stephanie's funeral." Lexie turned up her palms. "I guess I couldn't escape the gravitational field of the beach."

"Anna, Mark, and Brent needed help with the girls." Madison gave Olivia a sharp look. The local cousins had rallied, and she'd been conspicuously absent.

Point taken. She chewed her fingernail, feeling a little guilty. After all Anna and Mark had done for her, she hadn't dropped everything and moved back to Valencia Cove after the funeral. Her sister and brother, in Texas, wouldn't have been expected to help.

"Olivia had to consider Steele, and she had a job." Lexie placed a protective hand on her back. "Don't feel bad. We had it covered, and Anna's in bliss whenever Emily and Pixie are around."

She met Lexie's gaze with a silent thank you. "Are you still following hurricanes?"

"Yes. But this fall I had a temporary administrative position. My supervisor was on maternity leave. That's over. I'm back."

"Permanently?" She cocked her head. "Are working in the ER again?"

"Yes..." Lexie drew out the syllable with a mysterious half smile edging up her lips.

"She has a boyfriend." Madison arched a brow. "Who knows? She may finally settle down. The girls even met Zach. The guy at the bait shop who jumped in and saved Emily when she fell off the dock. Turns out he's Frank's son. He plays guitar... and he's a real hunk, with a charming southern accent too."

"Sounds interesting." She returned Lexie's smile. "How about you, Madison? Have you lost weight? Are you seeing anyone yet?"

"Me? Uh, no...not really." She waved off the question. "It's the stress diet. One day all salads. The next day cookies and sandwiches, whatever I can find in the hospital cafeteria. I don't recommend it." Madison lined the ingredients up on the counter in perfect order, utensils at right angles to the ingredients. Then she put measuring spoons and cups next to clean bowls. Orderly. Too orderly. This wasn't surgery.

"Is Kayden coming for lunch today?" Olivia washed her hands and tied on her apron.

"No. I'll get him tomorrow. I keep him alternate weeks. It's not easy sharing your child. But Emily and Pixie sometimes stay over." Madison released a long sigh. "I suppose that'll stop now that Brent's getting remarried and moving."

Olivia changed the subject. "Jennifer's coming, isn't she?" She kept up with the online photos of Jennifer's ceramics that her dad posted for her.

Madison loaded a paper towel and attacked a round pan, vigorously greasing it. "Dad's bringing her. Jen still lives with him."

"Time to get to work. I'll sift some flour." Lexie placed the contents of her tote bag on the counter and picked up a five-pound sack. She struggled with the bag. "What's with this? The top is so hard to open." She pulled with a good yank. The bag slipped to the counter. Flour puffed out and covered Lexie's face, the counter, and the floor at her feet. She gasped.

Olivia and Madison exchanged a look, then all three burst out laughing.

Lexie wiped off her face and started cleaning up the flour. She gave Olivia a playful hip bump. "Why don't the three of us check out the beach while you're here. Remember all those summers over at Crystal Sands?" A wide grin split her face. "Is your foot up to the beach?"

"If it means having a good time, I'm definitely up for it. It's been too long." Olivia passed her another paper towel for the mess.

Anna returned at the tail end of their conversation and gave them a meaningful look. "You three knew how to have a good time at the beach." Her jaw dropped. "Holy Toledo, what happened here?"

"Flour mishap." Lexie wiped the counter and floor. Flour still dusted the front of her hair.

"As clean as Anna keeps house, you could probably still use that flour." Olivia filled a glass measuring cup with sugar.

"Ugh. No thanks." Madison wrinkled her nose. "You know, the five-second rule is a myth. Bacteria—"

"I was kidding, Maddi...pedia." Olivia widened her eyes and caught Lexie's gaze.

Madison passed over the lemons. "Grate the peel. Juice the insides."

Olivia accepted the fruit, stunned at the authority in her cousin's voice. *Bossy much?*

"Let's plan on going to the beach while you're here." Lexie grinned. "I promise no skim boarding."

"You put the boys to shame, flying down the shore on those skim boards." Olivia washed the lemons.

Lexie chuckled. "I got their attention, didn't I? They always wanted to try it."

"I think it was your bikini the boys liked." Madison sifted powdered sugar.

"How would you know? You had your nose buried in a book under that beach umbrella of yours." Olivia finished zesting the lemon and squeezed out the juice for the lemon glaze.

Madison frowned. "If you freckled, you'd understand. Plus, you were busy sketching."

"When she wasn't fighting off the boys." Lexie wiped her wet hands on her apron.

True. She'd been happy in high school and had a few boyfriends. Lexie had a point. When did she start feeling so unappealing? Had Steele's routine criticism sapped her confidence that much?

"Remember the sandcastles we built with Jennifer?" asked Lexie. "We bordered them with walls made of those little coquina shells and filled the moat with seawater."

Anna greased a cake pan. "Stephanie loved tagging along. She always looked up to you three."

"Steph was easy, not like Jennifer." Madison frowned. "Dad made me bring her everywhere. I'm glad you were good sports."

"We loved having Jennifer." Olivia wrinkled her brow and caught Lexie's eye, she'd grown closer to her younger cousin, Jen, since they were both artists.

She tore off a paper towel and helped Anna grease the pans, falling back into the familiar rhythm, having baked with these women when they were children, and made these same cakes with their mothers and grandmothers.

The doorbell chimed. Lexie took off to answer it. Olivia followed, relieved to take a break from the commotion.

Jake stepped inside. "Hey, we're here."

"Hi, bro." Lexie threw herself into her older brother's arms for a hug.

"Hi, Jennifer." Olivia offered her cousin a quick squeeze and turned to Jake. "How's my *other brother*?" She hugged her other cousin, fifteen years older, closer in age to Anna, but taller and still had dark hair. "I had some of your holiday blend this morning. It's good."

"I aim to please." The café owner shrugged but seemed to brighten under the compliment.

"Jennifer, where's your dog today?" Lexie touched her elbow to her niece so she could follow sighted guide.

"Elton in the kitchen? While we cook?" Jennifer snorted. "Not a good idea. He may be a guide dog, but labs will eat anything. We'd be fighting him off or tripping over him." They moved to the kitchen. "I can tell the banana cake's made. It smells delicious. Is Madison here?"

"I'm at the table, breaking up chunks of chocolate." Madison glanced over. "Hi, Dad."

Jake touched Olivia's arm. "You have to come by while you're in town and see how Jennifer has the clay studio set up."

"That sounds like fun." She walked to Jennifer's side. The happiness she had for her cousin was edged with a touch of envy and she was glad her cousin couldn't see her face. Wouldn't it be nice to have a studio of her own?

Jake's voice filled with pride. "She has a lot of students." A couple of years ago, he'd bought the space next to his café, taken out a wall, and created Jake & Jen's Café & Clay. He strolled over and gave his oldest daughter, Madison, a rub on her shoulder. "How's my number one girl?"

Jennifer faced Olivia. "While you're here you should stop in and throw a pot."

"I'd like that. I'm probably a little rusty on the wheel. I've mostly taught 2D art, and I haven't been doing as much of my own art as I'd like to." A pang of regret hit her. She'd set aside her art and quilting time and time again to help Steele promote his portrait business.

"Remember that tea pot you made when we met up at the craft school that summer?" Jennifer puffed a laugh. "The teacher tossed it in the used clay bag, thinking it was a blob."

"I got better after that." Olivia gave her cousin a nudge with her elbow. "I'd love to have a pottery day."

"I'll show you how to make a dog sculpture. Those are selling really well." Jennifer's lips curved into a little smile.

She spoke around a slight lump in her throat. "That sounds like fun but I probably won't be here long enough to have anything fired." It'd be fun to make a dog figurine. If only it was as easy to sculpt a new life.

## 5

*A*nna glanced at the list taped to the cabinet and held back a scowl. Everything was timed out, and the plan was already collapsing. Cynthia was still missing, which meant ingredients were missing. Since Cynthia lived in Texas and seldom helped on cake day, she probably didn't understand the importance of being on time.

"So, what are we working on?" Jennifer sniffed the air. "Is the lemon cake baking? It's making me hungry."

"I just took it out." Anna placed an apron in Jennifer's hands. She and Madison had quilted Christmas aprons for everyone several years ago. "Let me help you get into it. I don't know why we made these challenging crisscross ties—half the time, I can hardly figure them out."

Jennifer ran her fingertips over the raised poinsettia on the front while she threaded the ties. She'd taken the time to outline the shapes on this apron with embroidery and seed beads, since her blind cousin couldn't see them.

"Jake, I'm glad you're here," Anna said over her shoulder. "Can you stick around for a while? Cynthia should be here soon with the coconuts and we need a strong coconut cracker." She struggled to keep the edge from her voice, but with these delays, they wouldn't finish until dinner time and she still had gifts to wrap.

"Is Blessie here yet?" Jennifer washed and dried her hands.

"She'll be here in a little while. Do you want a sample of batter?" Anna filled a spoon and touched it to Jennifer's fingertips.

"Save some for me." Jake reached for the bowl. Soon he was moaning with pleasure. "Anna, you're the queen of the kitchen."

She smiled. "If you're buttering me up to get more batter, it's working."

The phone buzzed. She wiped her hands and walked into the quiet of the living room. "Are you making the cakes? Is Olivia there yet? When are you coming to get me?" Blessie was anxious to come over.

A wave of guilt moved through her. It was easier getting started without her sister around. "Yes. We just started. Mark should be there any minute. Olivia and Jennifer are both here. And we'll wrap the presents you made when the cakes are finished—bring them."

Nearly twenty years younger and born with an intellectual disability and low vision, Blessie thrived in the environment Sacred Haven Center provided. Anna'd figured when their mom passed away, her sister'd live with her and Mark. In fact, she'd promised her mother she'd take her sister in, but it hadn't worked out. She returned to the kitchen. "That was Blessie. She's anxious for Mark to get there."

"Does Blessie still like it at Sacred Haven?" Using her delicate fingertips to check and make sure her measurements were accurate, Jennifer sifted a mound of flour, put two cups of it in a bowl, then measured and mixed in salt.

"Yes. There's a good horticultural program, sports, arts and crafts, even a therapeutic riding program." She studied Jennifer, who still lived with Jake despite being nearly thirty. "She loves the horses, and Mark even volunteers there. You could probably ride in their program too."

"I thought I heard something about financial mismanagement?" Madison drew her brow and met Anna's gaze with a frown. "They fired the general manager and are pressing charges. I even heard a rumor they might downsize the program."

Lexie cast her a warning look and loud whispered "Feeling Grinchy, Madison?"

"Yes, I heard something," Anna hedged, her head throbbing at the thought. Problems at Sacred Haven could spell trouble for Blessie. Mark would be fit to be tied if her sister didn't stay there. Dreams for carefree retirement travel would fall by the wayside. She amped up the cheer in her voice. "Time for music. Who wants jazzy Christmas, and who votes for country Christmas classics?" She'd concentrate on a lovely holiday and worry about Blessie and the center later.

Trevor swung open his door and welcomed the blast of cool air. Being outdoors with Molly always put him in better spirits. With the closing on the property moved up he needed a lift. Between the program tomorrow, the proposal he'd been working on, and the extra tasks associated with the holiday he was slammed. The terrier scampered to her water dish and collapsed on the cool floor, her adoring eyes following him. He pulled a jug of lemonade from the fridge, drank straight from the bottle. Why not? He seldom had a visitor.

The tiny stucco house he called home was like a monk's cell, with bare walls and few personal touches. An open book waited on the table next to a dark leather chair. The bedroom held a full-sized bed and an antique dresser. Photos of a pretty blond girl sat on surfaces throughout the cottage. Well-chewed dog toys, scattered on the floor, showed who truly owned the place.

A laptop, a calculator, and yellow pads with scribbles and numbers covered a coffee table. He'd been developing a full report of the cost analysis of the horticulture department. A copy of the budget with projections based on his plan might save the Center. It wouldn't only save his job but also enhance opportunities for the residents, a win-win if he could pull it off.

He checked his email but hadn't heard back from board members Mavis Willis or Seth Smith. With the closing changed, it was urgent. He cringed at the thought of slimy Seth with the fake smile. The way the creep looked down his nose at the residents got under his skin. How'd he get on the board, anyway? He huffed. Harris, the former administrator who was now facing charges, had appointed the jerk.

To some board members, simply keeping the lights on and safely housing residents was enough. Not him. This was his home, he'd spent fifteen years building quality programs. And he could lose it all.

With the holiday program tomorrow, he ought to shave, take a break from working and get a haircut. He peeled off his sweaty shirt and rubbed his hand over several days of beard. Despite sunscreen, laboring outdoors had tanned his trim body. Back when he'd been in finance, he'd monitored his diet and had gone to the gym. Now, mucking out stalls, working the garden, and going for long walks when he couldn't sleep gave him the fit body he'd aimed for in younger days. Vegetables, fresh from the garden, dominated his diet. *Not bad for forty-three.* "Isn't that the way it goes?" He scratched Molly, who'd made a bed from his filthy shirt.

He paused to look at the photo of his daughter on the dresser. Taken twelve years ago, Cherie'd come down for several weeks that summer. If they'd had the horses back then she might've come back. Sadness washed over him. His daughter had grown up calling his former friend Daddy, spending her holidays up north. Not knowing how much he loved her. He cursed and brought his attention to the present. After loading crates of produce for residents leaving for the holiday, he'd tackle his long list. The holiday program meant a lot to the folks at the Center and he wouldn't let them down.

Mark Hastings' new white Ram pulled into the driveway and parked near the pasture. Trevor waved. Good. He needed to talk to him. While Mark helped his two granddaughters out, he finished loading produce into a Ford pickup, then found the crates he and Blessie had packed that morning.

Mrs. Paulson, the stout gray-haired dorm parent, approached the truck and greeted Hastings. She took the girls' hands and the three of them walked over to the mini horse standing near the fence. Mark strode into the sprawling stucco building and short time later, the doors hissed open. He exited with Blessie at his side.

Trevor puffed a laugh—she was in her Christmas glory, wearing a glitter bedazzled reindeer tee shirt and blinking Christmas bulb necklace.

"Mr. Weston," she called over. "We had Christmas cookies. I like the chocolate candy cane ones the best. Want one?"

She held up a folded bag, a gleeful expression lighting up her face, and turned to Mark. "We sang 'Rudolph,' we sang 'The Twelve Days of Christmas,' and we put our arms in the air to make the five gold rings." She raised her arms high, forming a circle above her head.

"I know, Blessie, I know. That's why I waited to get you." Mark grinned and shook his head, smiling at Trevor. "If only I had her energy."

Trevor lifted a crate and hauled it to Mark's pickup.

Blessie shined a smile his way. "We're gonna make cakes, Mr. Weston. Olivia will be there too. I'm helping with the frosting. I can crack the eggs too." Her eyes grew wide. "Hey Emily, Pixie! Mark, I didn't know you were bringing the girls." She ran to the fence. They were squealing as Sundance's soft muzzle nibbled pellets from their palms.

Mark leaned on the truck. "You're too good to us, Trevor. Last time you had a big crate." He waved the girls over. "When will the games start up again? I can still coach."

"Great—you know we need you. The Saturday after New Year's, we have a game. Don't forget, we're having the annual staff versus resident's playoff."

"Sounds good. Count me in. And Anna wanted me to remind you to join us for Christmas Eve this year. No excuses. It'd mean the world to Blessie. Besides, Jake and I could use another man there. We're usually outnumbered."

"I appreciate the offer. Can I let you know tomorrow?" He gestured to a second crate. "Blessie wants this extra crate for cake day. She's been talking about it all week."

Mark nodded. "Thanks. Heard anything more about your job?"

Ordinarily he'd keep Center business close to his chest, but Mark was a reliable volunteer and had become a friend. "I'm here through January with no changes, but not sure how much longer. I may be out of a job. We're looking at cutbacks. The center lost some funding, and they plan to sell off acreage. I may take a hit."

"They can't let you go." Mark grimaced. "What'll happen to the horses? The garden?"

"Non-essentials." Tension set in his forehead. He crammed his hands in his pockets. "They need to keep the place going."

"What'll you do? Is there another position for you?"

"They mentioned part time." He shook his head. "Wouldn't be enough. But I might pick up hours working down at that garden shop." He nodded toward the road. "Silver Palms, the nursery on the other side of the railroad tracks, offered me a job."

"That stinks." Mark frowned. "Blessie's been excited about the garden and loves brushing the horses. With her low vision, she doesn't like the arts and crafts as much. You'll be able to stay on, won't you?"

"I'm not sure..." Trevor bit back his words. Blessie had returned and stood by the passenger door of the truck with a frown and a lowered brow, taking it in. Every word. His face heated. He cringed.

If he'd upset her.... He jerked his head toward her, and Mark got the message.

"Come on, girls, we're leaving." Mark turned back. "Let me know if we can help. Or if you need a reference. Anna and I appreciate what you've done for Blessie." He strapped the girls into their car seats.

"What's a reference?" Blessie asked, climbing into the truck.

Trevor watched them pull away. Mark sure had his hands full, but he seemed to love his family. Tightness caught his throat. Sadness? Regret? He fought it back and concentrated on loading produce into the next car. His family was right here, at the Center.

## 6

*O*livia kept a smile pasted on while she hammered her heel in irritation, wanting to get along, trying to enjoy the day. If Madison dictated any more instructions about how to break up the chocolate or separate the eggs for the meringue frosting, she'd scream.

Her cousin handed her a paper towel to grease the pans. "If you stick around, I'm friends with someone in human resources at Valencia Mercy. There may be a clerical job or housekeeping or C.N.A., but you might need to go for training."

Olivia pressed her lips together. She fainted at the sight of blood and wouldn't last five minutes working in a medical environment. Simply stepping inside a hospital made her queasy. Her degree was in art education with a master's in fine arts. *Try to focus on the good here, she means to help.* "Thanks, Madison. I'll keep that in mind." She popped a piece of baking chocolate in her mouth and winced at the bitterness.

Madison droned on and on, would probably run her life if given the chance. When had her cousin gotten so bossy? *Or have I become a first-class wimp?* Introverted and chronically underestimated, she might look incompetent, might even feel incompetent sometimes, but she wasn't. Did people think she had nothing good going on because she didn't share all her wins on social media? It'd taken strength to own up to how rotten her marriage had been and order the cheater out. Especially when everyone said she was lucky to marry a well-known artist. When would she learn to speak up for herself? If she'd found the nerve to be more assertive with Steele, it may not have gotten as bad as it had. Being agreeable worked against her.

Needing to rest her foot, Olivia escaped the chaos of the kitchen, sank into the living room recliner and put up her feet. Every muscle in her body thanked her. Then the doorbell rang. *Darn.* "I'll get it."

A smile sprung to her face when she found Tara on the sunny steps of Anna's house, sweat beading above her lip and a damp, red ringlet stuck to her forehead. "Tara." Olivia circled her cousin with a hug. "Hey, that looks heavy." She reached for one of the totes.

"Thanks. If I were in the heat any longer, this basket of eggs would hatch into chicks."

Leave it to Tara to have fresh eggs from her chickens. "Ha, well, the good news is we already have some cakes made. But this year we're also making three dozen decorated cupcakes for the program at Sacred Haven. Where're the kids?"

"I left Maya pouting. She refused to quit messaging her friends or even get out of bed and come along to cake day. Brian's working with Skip." Her husband ran a popular kayak rental business.

"Gosh, I'd love to get out on the water this week."

They rounded the corner to find Lexie and Madison spreading chocolate frosting on the cake.

"Yum! I thought I smelled fudge frosting. Hi, sis." Tara accepted a spoon from her younger sister, Lexie. "Mm. I needed this." She took a moment to lick the spoon then continued. "This year the kids are with us for Christmas, but it hasn't gone as I hoped—you know, making cookies, looking at Christmas lights, sipping cocoa."

"Cocoa! That's absurd. I wouldn't want that, either. It's ninety degrees out there today." Madison glowered, scraped the bowl, and handed the chocolate spoon to her dad.

"I know, but I'd crank down the air conditioning. Why aren't they happy to spend the holiday with their dad and me for a change?" Tara put the spoon in the sink and donned her holiday apron.

"Well, there's still hope. Christmas isn't over yet." Olivia surveyed the extended family crowding the kitchen. So different— these were her buddies, her cousins. Why'd she let Steele pressure her into staying away? With her next husband, she'd do things differently—if there was a next time. Lexie, Jen, and Madison were all single. What were her chances of finding someone?

A short time later, the ringing doorbell was followed by a loud rapping of the knocker. Olivia hung back as Tara went to the door. From the window, she spotted Cynthia tapping the pointed toe of a shiny red pump on the doorstep. Her older sister had arrived. She gathered a deep breath. *Stay calm.*

Tara swung open the door. "Cynthia, so glad you could come this year."

The woman held Tara at arm's length, kissed the air next to her cheeks, and flashed a tiny smile. "Someone locked the door? I'm perspiring. It'll stain my silk blouse." She gave Tara the up and down with a little frown. "It appears I've over-dressed."

Tara looked at her jeans and sputtered.

Cynthia strode over and gave Olivia a peck on the cheek. "It's been so long. Look at you." She frowned. "You look tired. Have you put on weight? I'll email you a copy of my juice fast."

Olivia opened and shut her mouth and groaned softly. This was why she'd chosen Tara for a confidant instead of her sister.

Cynthia marched into the kitchen. "I hope I haven't held you up too long."

Olivia reined in a smile, watching alarm flash across her sister's face. Flour, sticky batter, and frosting covered most surfaces. Cynthia glanced at her red linen skirt, dug into her tote, and pulled out a designer apron. She never wore her homemade holiday apron.

Anna shut off the water at the sink and turned to Cynthia. "Not to worry, Cyn, already started. We said nine. It's almost eleven. Did you bring the coconuts?"

"Coconuts? No. I picked up this dried organic shredded coconut. It's just as good, I'm sure."

"Don't worry about it." Anna smiled a tight smile. "Olivia's making a run to the store."

Olivia shot Tara a conspiratorial glance and slowly shook her head. Classic Cynthia.

"So, everyone's here?" Cynthia seemed oblivious to the head shaking. "Darlings, I brought a recipe for a lovely fig bourbon cake we can try it this year. Figs are the latest for baking." She reached into her butter-soft calfskin purse and pulled out a package of dried figs and the printed recipe.

Ever the diplomat, Anna glanced at the sheet. "We already have the baking planned, and I don't have any bourbon."

Cynthia raised her neck like a bird and looked around. "No Blessie this year? I imagine that's for the best. Bless her little heart, she tries, doesn't she? But let's face it... well, that means we can skip the candy cane cake and make the fig. I'm sure Olivia can buy bourbon while she's out."

Madison snapped her head around and squinted at Cynthia. "No! Blessie's on her way. These candy canes are for her and the girls to peel. We always make the candy cane cake."

Cynthia gasped. "Okay, dear, I didn't mean to offend. You know I want to help."

"How about greasing those cake pans or washing these bowls?" Anna suggested.

"Darling, I just came from the manicurist. How about a less hazardous task, hmm?" Cynthia held up her hands flashing a beautiful French manicure.

"Well, the carrots need grating for the carrot cake," suggested

Olivia. Again, Cynthia held up her hands to show her impeccable nails. *Leave it to Cynthia.*

"Okay, how about slice the tomatoes for lunch?" Anna tried again.

"That, I'll be happy to do. You know I'm here to help. But sweeties, I hope you won't be upset if I leave at noon. It's the only time Frederick can fix my hair. And I'm on a cleanse. I can't eat anything today, only powdered greens in distilled water."

"Timing, Cynthia. Did it have to be today?" Anna's smile was thin.

"Well, yes. The twenty-fifth we're leaving for the cruise. Does anyone have any gloves I can wear to slice the tomatoes? My, aren't these beautiful?" She lifted a large tomato.

"They're from Blessie's garden." Anna handed over gloves.

"Hm. She does enjoy playing in the dirt. It's nice they have that garden program." Cynthia held up the rubber gloves, inspecting them and wrinkling her nose.

Anna gaped, but then she agreed, "Yes, she loves the garden, but we aren't sure how much longer she'll have it. The program's at risk."

"Gosh, that's awful, Anna," Olivia chimed in. *No wonder Anna's been preoccupied.*

"That would be a shame for Blessie, but you can't stop progress." Cynthia held up the sharp knife then attacked the tomato.

Before Anna could reply, Mark opened the front door. "We're back." His voice boomed. "Come and see the two crates of produce. Did you save me some batter?"

Everyone gathered around, and Blessie showed off her harvest.

Olivia drew back, tensing when she overheard Mark speak softly to Anna. "Sorry, babe. Blessie heard me and Trevor talking. The rumors are true. They're planning to sell land, possibly close the garden. She was pretty upset, but I think I got her settled."

"Olivia! I got a ribbon for my strawberries at the fair this year."

Blessie smiled proudly, then slipped into a frown. "The garden. Mr. Weston might go to work at the garden store."

Anna brought Blessie her reindeer apron. "Let's not worry about that now when we need to make cakes. There are piles of candy canes that won't peel themselves." The group left Olivia, returned to the kitchen, and sounds of beating batter and baking resumed.

Olivia grabbed her purse and swung open the door. Her breath caught. There, getting out of a Jeep and approaching the door, was the guy from the photograph. She studied him. The man who'd fixed her flat. It had to be. In the daylight he resembled some actor she'd seen in a western. His thick head of sun-kissed light brown hair had a tuft that fell across his forehead. His skin, slightly lined and tan, had the texture of someone who worked in the sun. She could imagine running her fingers down his cheek and over the scruff on his jaw.

Despite the heat, he was wearing jeans, and the hot morning sun hit him from behind, making him appear to glow. Her gaze fell to his blue T-shirt, stretched across his muscular chest and arms, sticking from the heat. She lingered too long. When she brought her gaze up, his eyes sparkled as though amused.

"Excuse me," he asked in a deep voice and tilted his head. "Do I know you? This is the Hastings residence?"

"I think you..." she licked her lips, "... fixed my flat tire last night?"

A warm grin stretched over his face. "Well, isn't that something? Right. Glad to help."

Oh, boy. He was even better in person than in the picture. Strong, nice-looking, with a kind expression. His smile launched butterflies in her belly. For years, she'd been married to Steele with angular features and derisive tone. The man before her had an easy, friendly quality, charismatic.

The stranger continued. "I'm dropping these sacks off for Blessie. I'm Trevor Weston, one of her teachers. Mrs. Paulson said Blessie wanted to bring these today but ran off without them. I think they're gifts she means to wrap with Anna."

She stood silently for a beat, her mind blank.

The edge of his mouth kicked up and he raised an eyebrow.

"Oh, right. I'm Blessie's cousin, Olivia." She reached for the bag.

Blessie came bounding in and made a beeline for Mr. Weston, Anna trailing behind her. "Yay! You brought them. Thank you for bringing the presents. Anna, we need to wrap the presents, okay?"

Trevor handed the bag to Blessie with a smile that wrinkled the corners of his eyes.

Anna wiped her hands on her apron, gesturing to Olivia. "Trevor, I see you've met our cousin, Olivia. She's staying with us for a while. Please come in. We don't want to leave you out in the heat. Will you join us for lunch? We're in the final stretch of baking. I'm sure Mark would enjoy the company."

"Thanks, Anna. A glass of cold water would be great. It smells wonderful in here, like a bakery." He stepped inside. "I'd love to stay, but I've got errands to run for the program tomorrow. We're expecting a good crowd if the weather holds—storms should move through by late morning."

Olivia took a step back, but Trevor was still close enough for her to enjoy the fragrance of whatever he wore. Sandalwood? She leaned in. Nice.

Blessie returned with a glass of water.

Olivia studied him as he took the glass and drank. *Quit staring at him.* What was wrong with her? She hadn't even thought of dating since Steele had left and now, the man before her took her breath away.

Anna glanced at her with a curious expression and her cheeks heated. Could her cousin tell what she was thinking?

He handed his glass to Anna. "You're coming to the program, aren't you?"

Anna's gaze winged between Olivia and Trevor and she frowned just a little. "We'll definitely be there. Don't forget you're invited to our Christmas Eve gathering if you're free. Mark was supposed to ask you."

"He did, and I'll let you know for sure tomorrow, alright?"

A crash from the kitchen was accompanied by laughter from Pixie and Emily. Anna and Blessie returned to the kitchen.

Trevor caught her eye. "Are you the art teacher Blessie's been telling me about?"

"Yes, that's what I did in Tallahassee. I'm between jobs right now." Understatement.

"How long are you here for?"

"I'm not sure exactly. A couple of weeks." Her pulse picked up and her cheeks heated under his intense gaze.

"See you tomorrow night?" Trevor seemed like he wanted to say more.

"I'll be here," she croaked. *Say something—don't just let him leave.* No matter how much she wanted to sound smart or witty, the tangle of feelings working through her choked out all her words. "Thanks again for the help last night."

"No trouble at all." His gaze held hers for several seconds. He opened and closed his mouth without saying a thing, turned, adding, "Bye then," and headed back to his Jeep.

Olivia closed the door, leaned against it, settling herself. Good grief. She could get interested in this man. Already was, if her pounding pulse was any indication. Absolutely a bad idea. He's Blessie's teacher and she was heading to Dallas to live with her mother. Besides, who wanted a broke, unemployed divorcee, fast approaching middle age? Her hand touched her belly, soft from weeks of eating ice cream and chocolate like she was carb loading for a race instead of lounging on the sofa with her foot elevated.

She didn't need to be getting excited about Blessie's teacher.

Now was time to focus on launching Olivia 2.0, reinventing herself, earning money. Anxiety closed her throat. She took in a long, slow breath. *It'll be okay.* Like the book said, *"Focus on the positive, the little things to be thankful for."* Today was good. This moment was good. Whatever came tomorrow, it had to beat the mess she'd lived through the past few months.

## 7

*B*y four o'clock, sticky frosting and batter had been wiped off the surfaces and the scent of cakes and dish soap filled the gleaming kitchen. A pleasant feeling of connection bloomed in Olivia's chest. "It'll be nice to get off my feet and have a quiet evening." She'd been ignoring the twinges of pain flickering in her ankle.

"Yes. Get off those feet. You need to take it easy while you're here." Anna loaded the cupcakes into a box.

"Cynthia was such a diva and Madison was pretty crabby, but I think the day went well." She dried her hands and glanced at her cousin, who never seemed to run out of energy.

"I agree. Those two can be hard to take. But Madison's had a rough time since her divorce and it seems worse lately. When we get together to quilt, she's not so bad." Anna gave her a sidelong glance then opened the fridge and rummaged around. "How about salad and pasta for dinner?" She pulled out a pan of manicotti.

"That looks yummy. I can help with the salad." Olivia reached for the romaine.

"No. Sit. Stay off that foot." Anna's phone buzzed. She answered, her eyes grew round and she handed it to Olivia. "It's for you."

"Me?"

A woman identifying herself as Jeanette Bridges, Supervisor of Academic Programs at Sacred Haven Center, spoke crisply. "I apologize for the suddenness of this call. Mr. Weston was speaking to me and mentioned you're an art teacher."

"Yes." *What on earth could she want?*

"I know this is short notice, but we wonder if you're available to fill in here next week or longer. Classes are small. Many residents are gone for Christmas, but we still have programs going on a holiday schedule. We could use some part-time help in the arts and crafts room. We've been without an art teacher for a few weeks. Could you stop by to discuss it? This afternoon? I'm heading out of town for the holiday until Tuesday."

Fresh energy buzzed in her as she handed the phone back to Anna. "I have a meeting about a part-time job. Temporary, but I can really use the cash." She shrugged and gave her cousin a questioning glance. It'd take time away from visiting and she wouldn't be off her feet.

Anna lowered a disapproving brow. "Are you sure you want to do that?"

"I really need to." She dipped her head meekly and hurried to her room to change, excited about the possibility of earning some cash. Blessie rode back to Sacred Haven with her and told her all about the strawberries and horses. She listened with half an ear. With luck she'd run into Trevor there.

Olivia stood up straighter and focused on Mrs. Bridges. The interview had gone well. She gave silent thanks that she still had the proper credentials. A paycheck, even a small one, would help.

Jeanette Bridges, a solid woman with an air of efficiency as serious as her pewter gray suit, spoke in a no-nonsense tone. "Thank you for taking this on. As I said, it's temporary. We should have decisions about our programs by the end of January. If you can get us into the new year, that'd help." The administrator looked her squarely in the eye, then offered a surprisingly warm smile. "This means a lot to us. And you may call me Jeanette. We haven't been able to get someone part-time. Art is the highlight of the day for many of our residents, and some day students may also come in. Thank you for stepping up."

Jeanette showed her around the arts and crafts room. The spacious area had a shiny linoleum floor and smelled of pine cleaner. Labeled bins of materials lined shelves on one wall and cabinets over sinks lined another. She could remain seated in one of several rolling chairs part of the time, so her foot should hold up.

Along the far wall a bank of windows opened to the rear grounds with a view of a small stable and two cottages. Olivia spotted Trevor emerge from a cottage and head toward the building. She perked up, absorbed in watching him.

"What do you think?"

*I think he's what I want for Christmas.* Her cheeks heated with embarrassment, and she pretended to have been paying attention. "It's a great space."

"Take as long as you need to acquaint yourself with the room. The door's locked. Make sure it closes securely when you go. I'm leaving, flying out for the holiday, and have a plane to catch. Pick up your key Monday when you check in. Welcome aboard." Jeanette left.

They'd agreed Olivia would come in for the following week or two, afternoons only, and work with small groups, mostly paints and clay. She could do this. *Is that Trevor's voice in the hall?* Her stomach flipped with excitement. A glance toward the door showed him entering an office across the hall. She smoothed her hair.

The files and a black notebook on the desk commanded her attention. Here was information on the different students and their accommodations. Too much to cover now, she scooped up the notebook and folders, to take home and study. She'd have a better idea what she'd be doing come Monday. Bubbly anticipation lifted her spirits as she strode out the art room door.

The door clicked shut.

*Wait! My purse... across the room on the desk. Crap.*

Even though Jeanette had said it'd be locked, she tried the door, shaking the handle. *Darn.* She glanced up and down the empty hall. Mrs. Bridges' office was dark. Her keys were in the purse, locked in the art room. Staring at it wasn't helping. She shook the doorknob again.

"Is everything okay?" A deep voice startled her.

She turned to find Trevor standing behind her, more handsome than a teacher ought to be. The words almost got stuck in her dry mouth. "I'm locked out." She nodded toward the dark room. "I left my purse on the desk."

"I have a master key." He unlocked the door and followed her inside. "Jeanette didn't waste any time. I hope you don't mind me mentioning you to her. She's been trying to get someone in here for weeks."

He sat on the counter, arms at his sides, and gripped the edges which had the effect of drawing attention to his muscular arms. His legs stretched long in front of him, comfortable, confident. She could feel him studying her.

With some effort, she dragged her attention away from the man and focused on grabbing her purse. "I'm happy to help."

"We really appreciate it, Olivia." When he spoke her name, it was smooth and low and gave her shivers. "The arts program is important, and we haven't found anyone who'd even sub in the part-time position. Especially this time of year."

Her gaze roved over his broad chest, strong shoulders, and melt-me-now lips. Her heart picked up. She pushed her attention to the desk. If he'd noticed her attraction, he hid it well.

"A lot of the residents are off campus for the holiday. Activities are important for the folks who remain. Jeanette's great to work for. Just tell her if you need anything. And if you can't reach her, text me. Let's exchange numbers." Trevor locked his eyes with hers, "Again, thanks. I mean it."

She tilted her head and scrutinized this man who acted as if these people were his family and she was doing him a personal favor. They tapped their numbers in each other's phones, which seemed rather personal, but made sense. Notebook, folders, and purse in hand, she moved to leave. He held the door. When she passed him and brushed against his arm, her breath caught. Did he feel the same spark? She glanced away, her cheeks warming. When had Steele ever had this effect on her? One thing was sure, it hadn't been for a long time.

They stepped into the hall and strolled to the entrance.

"This is me." Trevor motioned to the right, then exited the rear doors.

Olivia watched him walk away for a few seconds, longing circulating inside her. Too bad she wouldn't be here past New Year's Day.

≋

Trevor raised his arms overhead, leaned back in his chair, and stretched out the tension. After hunching over his laptop for hours, the cottage had grown dark and his back ached. He'd checked his daughter's social media accounts and had sent her a quick Christmas message. Glad she was okay, his heart ached at the pictures of her living a full life that didn't include him. Rarely did he get anything but a terse response, so he tried not to get his hopes up.

He sent a few emails, checked his investments, and made notes. For the past week, he'd been hammering out a last-ditch effort to save the programs. Even though he'd gotten out of the brokerage business, he still managed his investments. Patience and strong nerves proved beneficial and paid off substantially when the market rebounded.

His parents would scoff. The family wealth didn't come from a few years in a strong market. But he took pride in being self-made, didn't rely on their money, and wouldn't give the satisfaction to his father. Which might be a mistake. Because he didn't have funds enough to bail out the center. Much of his savings was in a special account he kept on hand to help his daughter, Cherie. At the rate things were going, the Cherie account would earn a lot of interest, since they rarely even spoke.

He switched on the lamp and unfolded out of the chair, knees and back complaining from too much digging and shoveling and no days off. Holidays were a time to throw himself into work double time. It needed to get done—that's what he told himself.

Molly roused from her sleep, hopped to attention, and followed him as he opened the window and breathed in the muggy night air. She whined.

"Hey, girl, it's not morning yet."

A southerly wind kept the temperatures up until the cold front arrived and the delicate scent of the Mr. Lincoln roses he'd planted outside his window, drifted in. He stared at the midnight landscape, images of Olivia playing on his mental screen. She'd been on his mind last night after changing her tire. Even in the dark, he'd been drawn to her. Then she turned up at Mark's house. And what a surprise to see her in the hall earlier. Jeanette had immediately jumped on hiring her.

The instant he'd seen her at Mark's, something within him had stirred. Close enough to smell her floral scent, in that soft chambray shirt over tight pants, she'd woken up parts of him that'd been slumbering for years. With that olive skin and wavy dark hair, she was stunning. He'd been at a loss for words. Olivia was related to Blessie. How? They looked nothing alike.

He'd enjoyed it when she'd brushed against him earlier. In the art room, he'd fought back an urge to reach for her, and had kept his hands firmly anchored on the countertop so he didn't do anything stupid. But he'd wanted to, which wasn't like him at all. The edge of his mouth curved up. If he were honest about it, that's why he'd insisted on getting her number. Blessie's cousin was getting to him.

When Stacy'd left him for his best friend Raymond, and had taken his baby girl, his heart had been toast. He figured he'd eventually meet someone, but the pickings were few when you put in sixty-hour weeks working at a residential center for disabled adults and children. Tammi, the dining room manager, was interested. There was even that one night she'd shown up at his cottage door. It'd taken restraint to turn her away, and she'd been pissed. But he had to work with these people.

He'd constructed a wall around the part of his heart made for loving a woman and poured his energy into his job—an old story, but it worked for him. Caught up in the never-ending chores with the horses and garden, the sting of loneliness only crept in late at night or around the holidays. This year would be different. He'd accept the invitation to go to Mark's house. May as well, since his daughter hadn't responded to his invitation to come for Christmas.

The photo of a younger version of himself holding Cherie sat on the table by the window. She'd been about four. He could tell by the happiness on his face in the photograph that he hadn't had a clue what was around the corner. After the divorce, Stacy and Ray moved, and his daughter rarely made it down for her scheduled visits. He winced—he should've fought harder for her. He'd sent letters and gifts but had gotten no response and had paid child support even when he'd had to drive an old rust bucket of a car. Did she ever think about him? If he texted her, he got a one or two-word reply. It was like a knife in the gut, but what else could he do?

Trevor popped aspirin, chewed an antacid, and rubbed his neck, working out the ache in his head that continued to build. The situation, the finances at the Center, had been snowballing downhill ever since it'd come to light Harris had been siphoning off funds. Hopefully, members of the board would entertain a creative solution.

He bent down, picked up Molly, and scratched her back. The

wiry terrier licked his face, eliciting a smile. He set her down, leashed her, and they stepped into the night.

~~~~~

The moon lit the way as they moved past the garden. He stared toward the construction site and breathed in the smell of freshly cut lumber from the development, threatening his livelihood. He put his back to the blight and surveyed the grounds.

Colorful lights strung along the driveway and across the landscaping in the front of the main building still glowed, at least two hundred strands. He should know. He'd spent the day after Thanksgiving helping Edgar put them up. The smiles that lit up the faces of the residents made it worth the work.

He walked the grounds at the back of the property, stopping for Molly to sniff the air or look toward a sound. Possum, armadillos, bobcat, and foxes made the woods behind the cottages home. As the moon rose, he leaned against the rough split-rail fence. This vantage point offered a wide view of the night landscape. A screech owl broke the silence, then quiet blanketed them again.

Molly's ears perked up, and she whipped her head around. *What's that?* Trevor listened. *A car—no, a car door, even closer.* Was someone in the new subdivision? Construction sites were prone to vandals and thieves making off with supplies in the night. The terrier jumped to attention and growled. A moment later, the Christmas lights on the building blinked off. The timers were set for one a.m.

He froze in place. Molly continued growling. "Shh, Molly, hush."

Tension shot up his back as he peered at the main building. Is that a light in the business office? Straining to listen, he heard nothing and advanced a little closer, watching for the beam of light. If lights turned on and off in the dorm areas, that would add up.

This didn't. He scrutinized the office area. *Who's in there with a flashlight?*

He crept toward the building. Molly froze at attention and stared in the direction of the driveway, a low threat rumbling in her throat. Moments later, the dark shape of a car quietly rolled down the drive. About a hundred yards away, headlights came on. Nobody could get into the Center at this hour without knowing the code to the alarm and having a key. That was a fairly small circle. Dorm parents, he and Edgar, Jeanette, and the board members. Carefully inspecting outside the building, he found it locked up tight. *Hmm.* He stood in the driveway, looking toward the road, anger setting his jaw. Who would skulk around at this hour?

~~~~~

Back at his cottage, he sat at his computer and scanned the inbox. An email reply pinged in from the board president, Mavis Willis. *She's still up?*

*"Can you come tomorrow for a breakfast meeting? I suspect you're still up. Yes, it's a Christmas Eve breakfast meeting. Bring Molly too."*

Occasionally, the two of them had coffee and discussed the Center. Refined, but not afraid to put on garden gloves, she made mid-eighties look spry and pulled a few weeds with Blessie now and then. Every bit the dog lover he was, she reminded him of his grandma Paula, who'd taught him to garden all those summers he'd stayed with her growing up. He sighed. Still missed her. They'd spent many a happy afternoon with their hands in the dirt together. No wonder he enjoyed visiting with Mavis, who was about the same age Grandma Paula would be, had she still been alive.

He emailed back, *"Love to."* Tired, he pushed back in his chair and scrubbed his forehead, his busy mind refusing to shut off. *Why was that car on the drive by the Center?* The recent scandal had him suspicious, looking at the board members skeptically. Harris may not have acted alone, and the issue with the property sale seemed rushed.

He shucked his clothes and hit the bed. Within seconds, Molly jumped up and took her spot at his feet. Briefly, Olivia's face came to mind, her smile, how she stirred him. But less pleasant ruminations crowded her out. The mismanagement at the Center, would he be able to keep his job? Would he need to find a different place to live? Had that really been a light in the office? They needed to check the security cameras.

*a*t six-thirty a.m. on Christmas Eve, Anna was up peeling apples for her holiday specialty, traditional blueberry-apple breakfast cakes. If she mapped her day with military precision and powered through her to-do list, the day would unfold without a hitch. After dicing the apples, she added blueberries, squeezed a quarter lemon over them, took a deep whiff and smiled. She folded fruit into batter, topped them with cinnamon streusel and popped them in the oven.

An hour later, Mark sat at the table with coffee, milk, and warm blueberry-apple crumb cake. "This is so good." He moaned with pleasure. They sat in companionable silence, watching the red-bellied woodpeckers at the feeder. "I've gotta tell you. I don't think Olivia's going back to Tallahassee. When I unloaded her RAV, she even had lamps in there."

"I heard her saying something to Tara about her old roommate in Ft. Myers. But her friend has toddlers and not much room. I think she's planning to stay with her mom."

He hiked his brows up to his dark hairline.

"I know. I think it's a bad idea too. She and Aunt Lydia always do better from a distance." She cut him a sheepish glance. "What if she'd agree to move in with us?" They'd kept Blessie for a year after her mom had died and Mark had mentioned, more than once, how much he liked having only the two of them in the house now. The idea was to enjoy an early retirement together and travel.

"Do you think she wants to come back here?" His expression grew pensive.

"Would you mind?" She gave him more time.

Mark chewed and stared out at the backyard. "Don't get me wrong. I love Olivia." He sighed. "You know she always has a home here if she needs it."

"She should be out for breakfast soon. I can bring up the subject. If we travel, someone needs to check on Blessie. Besides, with the divorce, she isn't herself yet..." She allowed herself a small, satisfied smile. Caring was her area of expertise. "Olivia should move in for a while. Then this summer if we travel, she can house sit, look in on Blessie, and be around people who love her. Speaking of which, the way Trevor looked at Olivia —" she arched her brows, "—very different from the way he looks at his students. Definitely a spark I haven't seen before."

"She's a pretty woman."

"Right, but she's hurting right now. And he's probably eight or ten years older than her."

He puffed out a big breath. "I'm eight years older than you."

"That's different."

"If Stephanie were here, she'd probably tell you not to meddle. I know you mean well, but..." He touched her hand and gave her a pointed look.

She pulled her hand away, miffed. "That's a tall order when I can see plain as day what someone needs. Maybe you ought to tell Trevor to keep away from Olivia. You're friends with him." She'd also caught the way Olivia had reacted to Trevor. It seemed unwise for her cousin to get involved with someone so soon. It'd take time to get over that snake, Steele.

"Trevor's probably too preoccupied to think about Olivia with all that's going on."

"But she'll be working at the Center all next week. She's been through so much; I'd hate for her to get hurt." Anna snorted. Mark wasn't cooperating.

"I wouldn't worry. Trevor never dates. I suggest you stop fixating on this." He brought his hand to her face, smoothed back her hair.

She narrowed her eyes. "No promises." How would it be possible to keep them apart if they were both working at the same place?

Mark rubbed the bridge of his nose. "I think we ought to take a wait-and-see approach. He had a particularly bad divorce. Never saw much of his daughter. I don't think we need to worry. Blessie adores him and he's very good to her. Let's not rock the boat."

"I admit it's nice to have someone on the inside. It helps me sleep at night. But I don't need one more thing to worry about." She'd sleep well if she knew Olivia would be okay, even better if she knew the garden at the Center wasn't going under.

Olivia's heart jumped. She took a seat in the living room and listened. Anna and Mark were using their quiet, serious tone and talking about her. She couldn't hear exactly what they were saying, something about her boxes in the garage. Her chest sank. No way did she want to be a burden. She hadn't discussed needing a place to stay. Anna would feel obligated to take her in again. Plus, it was time she stood on her own two feet. She puffed a quiet laugh. That was a good one. With a broken ankle, standing on her own two feet had been nearly impossible for the past two months. This restorative stretch of time would really help. She'd be a perfect houseguest and use the vacation as a time to build her confidence so she could tackle her next chapter wherever that might be.

Their voices continued. She perched on the sofa. What were

they saying? Anna had definitely said her name. It wasn't so much she wanted to eavesdrop, but she didn't want to walk in and make things awkward. This would be a good time to do a calming practice she'd learned. She propped a pillow behind her back on the sofa, closed her eyes, and with the next few deep breaths, she concentrated on the comforting aroma of cinnamon and apples. Next, she tuned into the sound of the girls getting up and heading into the kitchen. After a few minutes, she switched to becoming aware of her body, letting go of tension, paying attention to her breath, allowing her hands to relax in her lap. Her mind slowly moved from sensation to sensation.

When a deep sense of peace spread through her, in drifted the image of Trevor standing in the doorway of the art room with a concerned expression. *Stop it. Focus. Fantasizing about Blessie's teacher isn't helping.* She brought her awareness back to the room and followed the sound of the girls into the kitchen.

"That coffee cake smells wonderful." She stroked a soft curl on Pixie's blond head and grinned at Emily, eating a piece of breakfast cake with a fork.

"Santa's coming," Pixie announced, shoving cake into her mouth with her fingers. "Daddy says Santa will come tonight, even at Rena's house."

"When Daddy marries Rena, will her parents be our grandma and grandpa too?" asked Emily.

"Probably," answered Olivia. "But Grandma Anna and Grandpa Mark will always be your grandparents no matter where you live, even if your daddy marries Rena. And I'll always be your cousin." She tenderly squeezed Emily's shoulder and glanced at her cousin. No doubt the situation was weighing heavily on Anna's mind.

She helped clear away the girls' mess. Anna wiped Pixie's hands and face and sent the girls off to pick up their toys. "Can we take our coffee into the living room, Olivia? I have something important to discuss."

"What's up?" She cradled her mug and took the chair next to the Christmas tree, breathing in its pine fragrance.

Anna launched into her pitch. If she'd stay, they could use her as a house sitter and to check on Blessie.

Her jaw dropped. Weren't there others in town to help with Blessie? It was tempting, and she wouldn't be beholden to her mother. But were they simply being nice? After living on her own for fifteen years, did she want to live with her cousins again?

"Think about it. No need to give me an answer right now."

"Can we revisit this after Christmas when I can think more clearly?" She adored Anna, but her cousin was pretty controlling, and she wasn't a kid anymore. Would remaining in Valencia Cove mean stepping forward or sliding backward?

Trevor was up early, having barely slept. So much was hanging on the meeting this morning. He rubbed his jaw, sore from clenching his teeth through the night, French pressed a coffee and fed Molly. The faint light of dawn was enough to guide him as he moved the remaining plants and pots into the greenhouse. Crispy brown plants were a damn waste if you could prevent it.

Blessie loved working in the greenhouse area, but it'd been a mistake telling her she could help this morning. The sun was barely cracking the horizon and no way could she be ready for at least another hour. He'd ask one of the dorm parents to tell her he didn't need her help this morning. It was enough of a challenge to get out the door before eight. As he hustled in the plants, Molly scampered around, hunting lizards.

Back in the cottage, he monitored the Center from his window. Volunteers were already arriving to set up for the special lunch and the holiday program. With luck, the storms would hold off until afterward. It wasn't only the rain, lightning put some residents on edge, and a loss of power could bring the entire production to a halt. But if the storms moved through early, the weather would be nice and cool for the program.

He texted Mark he'd come to the gathering, his heart picking up at the idea of spending time with Olivia. It'd be nice to have her around the Center. When he'd unlocked the door and followed her into the art room, he'd caught a whiff of her perfume and fought back the urge to ask her to dinner. He couldn't afford to get involved with so much at stake right now, but it'd be nice to hang out and talk with her. One evening with a pretty woman couldn't be that distracting, it being Christmas Eve, after all.

He changed clothes and gathered the financial files and his laptop. Despite the acid in his belly, he was optimistic. This morning they'd go over his ideas and, he hoped, nail down a rosy future for the Center and himself.

On the main drag, morning traffic was picking up. It moved smoothly as he drove toward the key, giving him time to stew about Cherie. He'd offered to buy her a ticket to fly down for a couple of days. *I don't get it. Can't she at least reply, even a couple words?* It looked like another year he wouldn't see her over Christmas. When he got through this mess with the Center, he'd find a way to connect, even if he had to fly up there.

Today's reading in her *No-Limits Holiday* book said, "*Do at least one random act of kindness.*" Easy—Olivia wanted to help. She'd do whatever Anna needed. Was that random enough? She found her cousin in the kitchen scooping meatballs onto a cookie sheet, the sweet aroma of breakfast still lingering in the air. "Do you need help with anything? In a little while I'm running out to pick up a few gifts."

"Maybe later. I have a schedule." Anna pointed to a list taped to the cabinet. "It's a good idea to get your errands done before the storms roll in. We're getting a cold front today." She glanced over with a bright smile. "We can finally break out our sweaters... Oh, you could deliver those cakes and cupcakes to church and the Center."

"Sure, I can do cake delivery."

Mark helped her load the cakes into the back of her RAV. At Peace Church, the secretary made a big fuss and thanked her for the three cakes. Next, she pointed her car toward Sacred Haven Center, where she'd drop off the candy cane cake and cupcakes, say hi to Blessie, and keep an eye out for Trevor. If he had time for coffee, she'd pick his brain about the different residents she'd be working with. She perked up at the prospect. Despite her better judgment, she wanted to see him. If she wasn't mistaken, that look he'd had on his face meant he'd welcome her visit.

She drove past the spot where she'd had the flat. Thankfully, Mark had taken her car in for a new tire yesterday afternoon while she'd helped with cakes, but it meant she owed him a few hundred dollars. It's a good thing she'd taken the temp job.

After passing the garden store, she bumped over the tracks and kept going. Whoa! She missed the Sacred Haven road, smacked the steering wheel in frustration, and had to make a U-turn, just like yesterday afternoon. The giant oak tree, a common landmark, was missing. She took it slower today and assessed the new construction, villas and houses replacing the woods and wetlands. The finished end was landscaped with identical groupings of pigmy date palms and red and yellow hibiscus bushes. This was the builder who wanted to expand over the east edge of Sacred Haven and threatened the garden Blessie loved. If she didn't know what a menace it was, she'd think they were attractive.

In front of the main entrance, she parked, balanced the cake holder on top of the box of cupcakes and carefully made her way inside. Anna would have her neck if she dropped this load. The entry doors hissed open and she inched toward a vigorous rendition of "Jingle Bells" ringing out of the large dining room. On the stage at the end of the room, a group was rehearsing, shaking silver bells. At the back wall, a thin, middle-aged blonde in skinny jeans and an apron arranged baked goods on a line of tables. Olivia approached her. The attractive woman had bright-red lips, heavy eyeliner, and wore a name badge labeled *Miss Tammi, dining room manager.*

The woman gestured Olivia to the end of the table. "Thanks for bringing these," Tammi cooed in a pleasant drawl. "Everyone loves that candy cane cake."

"It's our pleasure." Olivia scanned the room for Trevor. "The cakes are a family tradition that goes back for generations. The candy cane is Blessie's favorite."

"That's right. Blessie said someone would bring them. Honey, are you another sister?"

"Cousin. I'm Olivia. I'll be helping out here in the art program next week." Maybe she'd get to know this woman, since they'd be working in the same building together.

Either Tammi didn't hear her or didn't care as she looked past Olivia at a man who'd entered the dining room.

*Okay, now or never.* She tamped back the happy anticipation of seeing Trevor. *Keep your voice neutral.* "By the way. Would you happen to know where Trevor Weston is?"

The friendliness slipped from Miss Tammi's face as she assessed Olivia up and down with a little frown. Then she put the sugar back in her voice and responded with a chilly smile, "I do not know where he is. I saw him leaving his cottage with Molly before breakfast. They got in his car." Tammi's gaze narrowed. "I doubt he's returned. I haven't seen him."

Olivia tried to wipe the disappointment off her face, squirming a little under Tammi's scrutiny.

"I can leave a message, honey."

"Never mind. Thanks, anyway—it can wait."

Her cheeks burned, and she had the distinct impression Tammi was amused. She felt her brows draw together as she processed this information. Before breakfast he'd left his cottage with someone named Molly? A girlfriend? Anna'd said he wasn't married. Why hadn't the idea of a girlfriend crossed her mind?

Brushing against his arm had affected her like static electricity on steroids. Had she been so starved for a man's kind attention that she'd imagined the feeling could be mutual? He probably charmed all the women he met with that friendliness and his warm smile. Olivia 2.0 could handle this setback. She needed to make the cake delivery anyway, so, there was no harm done. But disappointment lodged in her chest like a stone.

Blessie waved vigorously from the second row on the stage.

Olivia pasted on a stiff smile and waved back.

"They'll be practicing another half hour if you want to hang around." Tammi smiled sweetly under flinty eyes.

"No thanks. I need to get on my way." She waved again at Blessie. Now she wanted to avoid Trevor, as though her hopes were etched on her face. She hurried out the door in case he appeared.

Palm trees and holiday traffic whizzed by as Olivia drove, sorting the tangle of thoughts circling in her mind. The whole Trevor thing wouldn't let her go. Twice yesterday, happiness had bloomed inside her when they'd been together. But his friendliness was probably a skill set cultivated from years of working with the people at the Center. She'd mistaken it for something more, had let herself have a little hope she might be desirable again. That was how far she'd fallen after living with someone like Steele.

Blinded by her ex's talent, she'd been flattered by his interest in her and had agreed to marry him but had made him wait until she wasn't his student. For years she'd supported his career and had placed her own art second, figuring she'd focus more on it later. Despite winning awards for her art quilts, he'd dismissed it as mere crafting.

She should've believed those rumors about Steele being a player. He was a repeat offender, and this last time she hadn't been able to look the other way. A baby was involved. That she even cared about seeing Trevor meant she was moving forward. *Now you know you're capable of being attracted to someone again. Thank Trevor for that.* Even if he was involved with someone else.

She pulled the car in front of Grace's Gifts and Wellness Center. Seeing Tara and doing some quick Christmas shopping would cheer her. To the north, dark clouds lined the horizon, and a flash of lightning streaked through the distant sky. With luck, she'd shop and be home before the storm arrived.

## 9

*B*lessie scowled and balled her fists. This day wasn't going right. Olivia had come into the dining room earlier and waved, but Mr. Perez, the music teacher, had given her a mean stare when she'd waved back. When Olivia'd brought in the cakes, happiness had filled her with smiles. She'd told Miss Tammi and the others she'd helped with the cakes, and the candy cane frosting too.

She'd wanted Olivia to stay for the rehearsal, hoping they'd eat lunch together. Then Olivia had spoken to Miss Tammi. She seemed sad and left. *Where'd she go?*

Distracted by her worries, she sang out before the others and earned another sharp glance from Mr. Perez. It was hard to pay attention to him. Instead, she worried about Mr. Weston. She was supposed to help him this morning and usually saw him in the dining room having coffee with Miss Alma.

This was supposed to be the best day ever. She'd help in the greenhouse, practice singing, have the special holiday lunch, and then would be the program. There'd be a skit too. After the program, she'd hand out cookies at the refreshment table. Then she'd get her suitcase and go to Anna and Mark's house. Playing with Emily, Pixie and Lindsay would be fun. They'd watch Rudolph on TV. Then the cake party. Christmas was the best time. Plus, there'd be presents. She'd made potholders in the craft room before their teacher had left. She'd used loops on a thing called a loom. It'd been hard, but they were pretty.

The rehearsal ended early allowing free time before lunch. She ought to find Mr. Weston and see if he still needed help. Her face tightened with worry. They were supposed to move the plants after breakfast. It might get really cold tonight and kill them. He'd told her yesterday she could help him this morning.

She searched all over the dining room and even checked the kitchen. It smelled so good. They were roasting the turkey for lunch. The cooks told her to get out of the kitchen and not bother Mr. Weston.

Next, she wandered the hall of the main building and peeked in the office. He wasn't there. She checked in the media center and walked down the north dorm wing. Nope. What about the south dorm wing? Not there, either. Near her room—she might as well get her old sneakers on and walk outdoors to look around.

Her pulse picked up when she cracked the door to the stables, nervous. She wasn't allowed to go in alone. She crept in, calling for Mr. Weston. The horses, Sundance, Brink, Winnie and the new horse, Sandy, stood in their stalls. Sundance nickered, stepping toward her. The mini horse was her friend and wanted her to pet him. "Not now, Sundance."

At the edge of the property in back, Mr. Weston and Mr. Edgar had cottages. She spotted Mr. Edgar's blue pickup truck leaving his cottage, and froze, waiting a moment so he wouldn't see her coming out of the stable. When his truck moved down the driveway, she stalked out to the back fence where Mr. Weston usually walked Molly. Not there. What about his cottage? It was off limits. He had privacy. If she found him in the garden, the greenhouse, or the main building, it was okay to talk to him. "Don't pester him all the time," Anna had warned her.

She surveyed the entire back area. Nobody. People inside were getting ready for the program so no one would notice her break the rule. Her heart quickened as she hurried across the yard to Mr. Weston's cottage. It might bother Mr. Weston but she knocked on the door anyway. Quiet. She knocked harder. Nothing. Not even Molly's bark. Where was Molly? Did something happen to her? Did something happen to Mr. Weston? She pounded the door. No answer. Her breath caught. *They're missing.*

*Could he be walking Molly around front?* She marched around the building and started down the driveway in the midday heat. Sweat ran down her face. She wiped her forehead on her shirtsleeve. At the entrance, she checked up and down the road and frowned. Then it hit her. Mr. Weston might be working at the garden store Mark had shown her. He probably needed to move the plants there too.

Her lip trembled. He might have a job there and not be at Sacred Haven anymore. Mr. Weston always had jokes for her and never lost his temper. Today he'd help set up for the program too. She'd go to him, help him, and tell him to hurry back. Mark had shown her the garden store. It didn't seem far, but she'd need to cross the street. People pushed a button and crossed at the light. She'd find the button, then find Mr. Weston.

The long, curving driveway led out to the road. *It's so hot. Why didn't I get a drink of water?* There wasn't a sidewalk, so she needed to be careful. A tall gray bird stood very still in the water-filled ditch. The gray ones were pretty, but the pink birds called spoonbills were her favorite. She palmed the sweat off her forehead.

A silver car passed her. Not Mr. Weston. His car was black. She kept going until she reached the main road. Mark always turned toward the railroad tracks in the distance. She hustled in that direction, using the sidewalk. To her left, traffic moved quickly. On the right, a pond full of tall grasses called cattails stretched a long way. She stepped up her pace. There could be an alligator in there. A truck rumbled by, and she stopped, afraid. The sidewalk was too close to the road. She froze in place, unsure if she should go on, stuck between traffic and the pond.

Hard pounding in her chest reminded her that she was breaking the rules by going alone. Mrs. Paulson had come with her the few times they'd walked to the little grocery store in the other direction. Her dorm parent had said to be careful of getting too close to the road and never go by herself.

What time had she left? It must be getting close to lunchtime. Her chin set in determination and she picked up speed, moving swiftly past the pond. She needed to get back before lunch.

～～～

Trevor's tension eased by a degree when Mavis stepped out of her stately beachfront home with a warm greeting. This woman might hold the key to the messed-up situation. Despite her beautifully tailored pants and blouse that'd likely cost more than a week of his wages, she bent down and scooped up Molly.

"How's my girl?" The terrier covered her hand with licks. A grand old woman, beautiful with silver hair swept up in a clasp, her sorrowful brown eyes contrasted with her pleasant greeting.

He followed her into a home opening to an expansive view of the crashing gray-green gulf.

"Let's eat first. You sit over there." She waved Trevor to the seat facing the water through floor-to-ceiling windows. "Jean-Pierre's outdone himself. I'm afraid he's made enough to feed an army." She gestured at the spread.

His mouth watered.

Jean-Pierre appeared with two small bowls for Molly. "Would your dog like water and sliced chicken breast?"

"Thank you. Just a tiny amount of chicken." He turned toward the spread while Molly licked the bowl clean and slurped water. "You and Jean-Pierre will make me fat." They sat down to a delicious breakfast of crepes, eggs benedict, sausages, sliced tomatoes, a variety of pastries, and finished it with fresh whipped cream over strawberries.

Mavis had a stocking stuffed with chew toys and dog treats for Molly. And she gave him a box of delicate cut-out cookies garnished with marzipan in the shape of Christmas ornaments. He presented her with several small jars of dried herbs from his private garden.

Jean-Pierre, Mavis's private chef and personal assistant, brought them espressos. He'd insisted on staying through early afternoon until her family arrived and got settled before going home to his own family.

"I probably owe my life to Jean-Pierre. He's been with me almost thirty years. And he's forced me to keep eating. I'm afraid my appetite isn't what it used to be since I buried Rodney."

"He's a wonderful chef. But if I eat much more, I'll explode," Trevor kidded while he polished off a second flaky croissant slathered with Irish butter. *She probably thinks I haven't eaten in days.*

They drank coffee and watched laughing gulls swoop the breeze and light on her patio. She pointed out the window. "Look, over there." About fifty yards away, a pod of dolphins rose out of the water. "They go deep during storms. Since they're rolling, we probably have a while before the squall lines arrive."

He grinned, watching the marine mammals surface and dive. It seemed a good sign for his meeting. "Your view can't be beat."

"I do love to watch the storms roll in off the gulf."

They sat in quiet for a long moment, comfortable together, enjoying the view.

"This first Christmas without Rodney's been rough. We would have celebrated our sixty-first anniversary last month." Mavis paused and confided, "I didn't think I could go on. But Jean-Pierre kept at me to get back out there, saying my life still mattered and I could make a difference at the Center. It helped. Sacred Haven's been like another child to us, and I need to keep going to take care of it. Especially lately." She gave Trevor a knowing look.

"I'm glad you're more involved. The residents really care for you. Plus with the chaos from the situation Harris created..." He gestured, palms up. "I don't know how we'd get it all sorted out without you." Rodney and Mavis had been the backbone of the Center. When one of their grandchildren had been born with Down's Syndrome, they'd become advocates for people with disabilities, embraced philanthropic work, and launched Sacred Haven.

The two moved into the sunroom where he could lay out the files, open his laptop, and go over his proposal. His chest lifted with hope the plan would appeal to her. A sharp woman who still had a lot of energy, she helped sustain the Center with generous donations, volunteer hours, and an annual gala. The Center was getting ready to celebrate its 25<sup>th</sup> anniversary and offered residents more programs than ever. Until Harris.

"Why don't you show me what you've come up with and we'll determine if it's ready to present to the board. I know things look like they've gone to hell. With all the traveling Rodney and I did before he passed away, we weren't paying close attention to Harris. That crook looked so good on paper. Things have gone downhill, but it's not too late. I'm not in favor of the plan to sell the acreage. It's too big a price to pay, considering the programs we'd lose." She arched a brow at him. Her words were encouraging, but they had other board members to convince and needed a solid alternative.

"By the way, we found someone to fill in the art room for a week or two."

"Good. I'm against the proposal to staff the arts program with volunteers." Her faced pinched. "We need at least a part-time certified person in the position."

The doorbell rang.

"That'll be Grant Taylor from Granite Solutions Investigators. I asked him to come for the meeting."

"You hired an investigator?" His raised his brows. He'd met

Grant through his friend, Brice, and had heard good things about the new agency.

Jean-Pierre led Grant into the sunroom. After pleasantries, the investigator got straight to the point. "Smith's connected to the developer. They have an association going back several years. And Harris was tied to it too. I'll need to surrender these findings to the sheriff. It may tie in with the embezzlement. I'll keep you updated."

Mavis scowled. "Smith was all for selling without considering the effects it'd have on the residents. It doesn't surprise me he's got some underhanded dealings going on. He's an idiot. Doesn't interact with the residents, only looks at the budget. I don't understand how he got elected to the board. I'm sure it was Harris's doing while Rodney and I were on that cruise. The folks need the arts and crafts and love the horticulture program. And the community at large benefits from the therapeutic riding program. We're meeting the needs of all the residents better than ever."

Grant launched into an explanation of what he'd uncovered. Trevor groaned. Scandal reduced community support. But if it meant getting Smith off the board, they might be able to swing the other votes and rebuild trust.

When he left, Trevor's step was a little lighter. There was hope. He and Mavis were on the same page. Now he could head back to the Center for a pleasant holiday afternoon. He laid his blazer across the back seat. T-shirts, jeans, and snake-proof boots were standard in his job. But for this morning's breakfast with Mavis, he'd pulled on chinos and worn a jacket over a tailored button-down, and his favorite leather boat shoes. Molly hopped in the driver's door and scampered to the passenger side, where she put her paws on the window and barked at the leaves picked up in the breeze. He snapped her harness to the seat belt. A charcoal sky threatened and he cursed the clouds rapidly moving in from the north. They weren't gonna beat the rain.

Before pulling out of Mavis's circle driveway, Molly whined, cast him a pleading stare. "Sorry, girl." He scratched the side of her face. "You can't ride in this traffic with your head out the window."

Holiday drivers filled the road, entering and leaving the key. Over the rail of the bridge, he spotted whitecaps whipped up on the bay and waves pounding the seawall. Large drops started pelting the windshield. Molly's eyes went wild as she panted.

"It's okay, girl. Calm down."

The meeting had gone as well as he'd hoped, but it was too soon to share the news. Mavis would contact the other board members this afternoon. Yes, it was Christmas Eve, but this was urgent. They'd tolerate a holiday intrusion from Mavis, whose wealth and age allowed her to play the eccentric card. A meeting was planned for the afternoon of the twenty-seventh, allowing time to rework the deal for the proposed closing on the morning of thirty-first.

A rumble, long and low, interrupted his thoughts. The sky opened up. Molly whined. To calm her, he found relaxing music on the radio and raised the volume. Water already pooled at the edges of the roads. Not a problem—his Jeep could get through it. He drove slowly, navigating the back roads, but visibility was almost zero. He pulled over to wait in a parking lot. The squall lines should move through within the hour, and then they'd have blessedly cool weather for Christmas Eve.

In the meantime, it was torrential. Bolts of lightning flashed, almost as bad as a summer storm. Molly panted and whimpered, straining against the seat belt holding her harness. He reached over and rubbed his thumb across the top of her head. "I know, girl. I know. We'll be home soon." It'd be a relief to get her indoors. At least he got all the plants into the greenhouse.

The greenhouse.

*Blessie!*

He'd forgotten all about her. How could he forget to tell Alma that Blessie didn't need to help with the plants? And now it was storming. Maybe the rehearsal would keep Blessie occupied and distracted from the storm. She had storm hatred as bad as Molly. Here on the west coast of Florida, lightning was intense. Back in June, it'd struck a tree on the grounds, starting a small fire. The fire department had been called. Since then, many of the residents were more frightened than ever when it stormed.

After about twenty minutes, the rumbling moved to the distance and the rain let up enough to drive. He restarted the Jeep. Before putting the car in gear, his phone pinged. A text from Alma: *Blessie's missing. Looked everywhere. Is she with you?*

His breath caught. *With me? Missing? What the...?* He called Alma.

"We can't find Blessie. Did she ride somewhere with you?"

"No. I've been at a meeting."

"We've searched all over. She wasn't at lunch." Alma paused. "Do you think we should call 911?"

"She wasn't in the greenhouse or in the garden? Did you check the stable?"

"Yes. No, she's nowhere. We checked all over."

"Call 911. I'll be on the lookout for her as I drive back." He put his car in gear and sped in the direction of Sacred Haven.

The pounding of Blessie's pulse filled her ears when she found the crosswalk at the traffic light and started across the five lanes of traffic. Everyone stopped like they were supposed to, but it seemed shorter when she crossed with Mrs. Paulson. There were so many cars. She turned back once, changed her mind, and headed toward the other side. An angry man yelled and honked his horn.

Once across, she surveyed the area and tried to figure out which way to go. Her lip trembled. Despite wearing her thick glasses, it was confusing—everything seemed different on this side of the road. She couldn't make out the words on the yellow-and-white signs. She spotted the train tracks and headed that way. What was that ahead? Relief washed over her as she recognized the large red sign of the garden store in the distance and stepped up her pace. Dark clouds were moving over the sun.

Gusts stirred up debris from the edge of the roadway. Loud rumbling moved in from the distance, the sky growling. As the wind picked up, large drops of rain hit her arms and lightning cracked across the sky overhead. She ran for her life as the thunder shook everything around her, booming and crashing. *The garden store.* She tore through torrential rain past the two cars in the parking lot, heart pounding like a creature trying to escape her chest. A deep puddle blocked the entrance. She nearly slipped. When she reached the awning, she slowed, got inside, and stood looking around, gasping and shaking in the air conditioning.

At the checkout with his back to her, a man talked as he bagged purchases for a woman in a raincoat. "Silent Night" softly played in the background. The man turned toward Blessie and called out, "We're closing soon, ma'am. Early hours for Christmas Eve." Then he continued bagging and talking to the woman, who was laughing.

Blessie turned away and scanned the store. Crash. Lightning flashed right through the building, blinking off and on the lights.

The woman at the register took her bags. "My, that's a close one. Let me wait in here five more minutes." She and the man started talking about the rain.

The sound of their voices faded into the background as Blessie moved toward the back of the store. She peered to the left and right down every aisle but didn't see Mr. Weston anywhere. Off to the side, glass double doors lead to an outdoor area filled with bushes and plants. A rack of bright red poinsettias stood close to the door, and tables of red, yellow, and pink flowers in small containers stretched from one end to the other. Large bags of soil and mulch in tall stacks made their own rows. Mr. Weston would probably be out there. He liked the plants, and she'd seen him carry those bags of soil. She moved through the glass doors.

There was no roof, and she got soaked while she surveyed the area. Nobody else seemed to be outside. She walked toward the stacks of soil and mulch. Another fork of lightning arched through the dark sky as thunder shook the building. Boom! She shrieked, ducked her head, she ran in between the stacked bags. A plastic cover made a tent over these, and it was dry, quiet, and safer in this place. More thunder. She crouched down. If lightning were going to strike, it helped to get as small as you can. She pushed herself back into the bags and became a little ball. Now the lightning couldn't get her. The smell of the soil was soothing, like the garden. Until the thunder stopped, she'd wait here, then find Mr. Weston.

To stay calm, she sang softly, "Rudolph the Red-Nosed Reindeer," "Jingle Bells," all her favorites. It didn't help much. Finally, the rumbling moved into the distance. Her stomach growled. Was she missing lunchtime? She thought about all her favorite lunches. Grilled cheese was at the top of the list. Tomato soup and grilled cheese would be so good right now. Then she remembered. Today they were having a special holiday lunch with gift bags for everyone. And open-faced turkey sandwiches with cranberries. Cranberries grew in a bog, not a garden. Cranberries wouldn't grow in the Sacred Haven garden. *The garden!* What if they took her garden? Her heart jumped to her throat. She had to find Mr. Weston.

Water dripped from the gutters and roof, but the rain had stopped. She peeled back the plastic and ventured into the open garden center where bright rays of sunshine beamed across a mess. Plants lay on their sides. Dirt spilled out of containers, covering the concrete. Mr. Weston wouldn't like that. "Clean it up," he'd say.

Blessie called out and checked around. He wasn't out here. She moved to the door she'd come through. Locked! Dark, no lights on at all. She pounded on the door and pressed her face against the cold glass, searching inside. *Where'd the man go?*

She surveyed the outdoor section. A big chain door closed off the area beyond the cash register. Blessie ran to the door and tried to open it. *Oh no, the door won't open.* She stared down at the padlock in disbelief, wove her fingers through the rough metal links, and shook the door.

A chilly wind blew through the garden center. Soaked and shivering, her teeth chattered. Despite the blue sky, it was colder than ever, the temperature dropping fast. She clenched her teeth, snorted, crying and screaming at the same time. She ran up and down the aisles past tables of plants and tipped-over bushes, then slipped on a broken pot, falling flat to the concrete. Her palms stung. The broken pot had ripped a hole in her pants, cut her shin, and blood dirtied her pants. She wiped the blood with her hand, brow gathering as she checked the cut—not too bad, but it was messy and hurt. *Darn it.* They were her new pants for the program. She took a moment to hold the fabric over the cut and stop the bleeding. She needed to go to the clinic. But the clinic was back at the Center.

*What happened to the man working at the cash register? Mr. Weston's not here, either.* All alone, locked in, she could even be missing the program. She trudged over to the short stack of mulch bags, sat, pressed her pants against the stinging cut, and let out a wail.

## 10

*A*nna rolled her shoulders, fighting the tension of too many last-minute things to do, typical for Christmas Eve. If she wasn't always combing through magazines and the Internet for recipes and decorating ideas, life would be simpler. She hummed along with her playlist of carols and put finishing touches on gifts, easier with the girls gone. Before the rain started, Lexie had picked up the girls for cut-out cookie day and would meet them at the program.

She mentally reviewed the to-do list. At least the cheese was on a platter and the meatballs in the crock pot. Wouldn't it be a nice change not to race around, stressed out right before everyone arrived? With Olivia's help this afternoon, they'd make it to the finish line before heading to Sacred Haven for the program.

The Christmas cakes covered the long table in the living room. Little lights twinkled in greenery bordering the tablecloth, and candles were artfully placed in the middle, like a decorating magazine centerfold. It was shaping up to be another award-winning holiday.

Anna took her final package and set it under the tree. Olivia'd returned, complaining about the storm, and was fixing her wet hair and changing clothes. As the weather cleared, it should be beautiful, cool, sweater weather. She'd change into a Christmas cardigan that matched her new dress, the one with holly embroidered at the neckline.

Her cousin stepped into the room, holding arms full of small gifts.

"Wow, you had good luck shopping, didn't you?" She adjusted her gifts so Olivia could place the presents under the tree. "Look how gorgeous you are. Is that top new?"

"Yes!" Olivia beamed. "It was on sale. Tara helped me pick it out. Unfortunately, I had to put the brace back on my foot, so I can't wear my heels. I was on my feet too long and it was aching again."

*Is Olivia overdoing it?* It was probably too much for her to deliver the cakes. "Why don't you sit down and let me wait on you for a while?" She motioned her cousin to the sofa. "Do you want some cocoa? And how did you find time to get so many gifts this morning?"

"They're all from the shop where Tara works. She helped me choose them. Amazing, right? She helped me wrap them all at the shop. I'm set." Olivia sat down and continued. "Tara gave me a cup of one of her new tea blends, said it was anti-inflammatory. I bought some for Cynthia. She's so difficult to buy for."

Anna agreed. "It is hard to choose for some people. We're so blessed. We have what we need." She picked up a box Olivia put under the tree, turning it around, and continued, "I love the foil wrapping you did with the sprig of baby's breath. You know, I'm a bit of a gift-wrapping snob."

"No, you aren't a snob," Olivia argued with a grin. "Well, maybe a little." She leaned back on the sofa and lifted her foot to the top of the ottoman. "You're just good at it, Anna. Teach me how to make those incredible bows when you have time."

She allowed herself a satisfied smile and laid out her enticement. "If you stay, we'll have lots of time to do crafting and baking."

Her phone buzzed. "Hello."

"Hi Anna. This is Alma form Sacred Haven. Blessie's not with you, is she? Did anyone pick her up?"

Her heart jumped to her throat. "What? No! What do you mean? Did you check with Trevor?"

"She's not with him. We called the sheriff." There was a pause. "You may want to come over."

Her fingertips turned to ice. Panic gripped her chest.

Olivia sat up, her expression alarmed. "What's wrong?"

She pocketed her phone. "Mark! Mark, we need to go. It's Blessie. She's missing. They thought you may have picked her up." She searched Olivia's face. "You haven't seen her, have you?"

"No! No, she was on the stage practicing when I left the cake off."

"They wondered if she rode somewhere with Trevor but got him on his cell. She's not with him. He's on his way back now, looking for her."

Mark bolted into the room. She repeated what she'd learned on the call. They grabbed their jackets. "Miss Alma said they hadn't seen Blessie for lunch. She wasn't in her room. They'd started searching for her. Nobody can account for her since the rehearsal. They said to come right over. The sheriff's already been called."

She ran toward the pickup, Olivia and Mark piling in right behind her. Olivia texted the other cousins while Mark sped along. They scanned the sides of the road. She brought a hand to her chest as though it'd help her breathe. "Blessie wouldn't try to walk to our house, would she? Especially in the storm."

Mark squeezed her hand, his face hard. "I doubt it. At least the rain is letting up."

"Blessie probably knows the way to our place—it's a straight route down the road from the Center. But why?"

"It's several miles. I can't imagine her going that far." Mark turned off the wipers.

"No, I don't think she'd come here. The Center was having a

special lunch, and she knew we were coming over for the program. That wouldn't make sense." She swiped a tear from her cheek.

"Blessie hates thunderstorms, would never go out in a storm. Unless she went somewhere before the storm." Mark's jaw ticked.

"Is it possible she's there on the grounds somewhere, hurt? Do you think she got bitten by a snake? She could be unconscious with a bite from a rattler or a coral snake, or even a gator." She could hear the desperation in her voice.

"It won't do any good to panic, Anna," Olivia piped up from the back. "Don't let your imagination run wild. Take a deep breath. We'll find her. She wouldn't go far."

Mark reached over. The weight of his large hand enveloping her icy fingers was small comfort. "Sweetheart, it'll be okay. It's not like Blessie to disappear, especially right before an event she's been looking forward to for so long."

It was bad enough losing Stephanie. She couldn't handle it if something happened to Blessie too. Olivia reached up from the back seat and patted her shoulder.

Mark drove too fast, but they got there in one piece. They jumped from the truck.

"You go in ahead," urged Olivia, limping and stepping gingerly around puddles.

A crisp winter breeze blew under a crystal-clear blue sky. The temperature was dropping fast. Mark ushered her toward the entrance, bringing his jacket around her. She couldn't stop shaking.

Trevor parked next to the squad car, noting a deputy sitting inside on the radio. The other deputy stood behind the glass doors of the main entrance to the Center, talking to the small group. Almost oblivious to the bracing cold wind, he sprinted to the doors with Molly scampering at his heels. Determination had every muscle in his body tense. He needed to make this right.

The officer with Deputy Daniel Jones on his shirt was asking questions, taking down notes, bringing Anna, Olivia, and Mark up to speed. Mark was anxious to get on the road to continue the search.

"Slow down, sir. We'll get out there. I'll need a photo and a few more answers first," said Deputy Jones. "She wouldn't take one of the vehicles, would she? Is there anyone else who may have picked her up?"

Mark and Anna both answered, "No!"

Trevor checked in with the group. He put Molly's leash in Miss Alma's hand. "Hold her, okay? I'll be back in a few minutes. Let me run out and recheck the greenhouse and the pond." Guilty feelings weighed heavy as he blamed himself. Distracted, thinking about the meeting with Mavis, he'd taken care of the plants alone and had likely confused her. When he made a plan with Blessie, he was always right there, on it. She could count on him. He'd let her down.

Where would she go? She wouldn't miss lunch and the program unless she's hurt. Heart jumping in his chest, frantic, he searched the back part of the greenhouse. He ran all the way down the greenhouse aisle, checking between the rows of shelves and tables.

"Blessie, Blessie are you here?" It wasn't like her to kid around. Something was wrong. No sign of her. He left through the side door and sprinted around back. No Blessie. Next, he circled behind the cottages and even checked the pond. Years ago, a resident had nearly drowned in the pond. A short fence had been built. She wouldn't go in the water. There were snakes and likely a gator. He studied the surface anyway, chest tight, paying attention to the area at the back where the reeds were thicker. There was no sign of her in the pond. Thank God. He released a breath he didn't know he'd been holding.

Cars were pulling in and parking for the program. He checked the time. *Crap.* That was happening soon. Heart hammering, he cursed and took rapid strides to the main building.

He approached the officer. "Deputy Jones, we have video surveillance as part of the new security system. There's a camera on the entrance. Have you checked it yet? I'm pretty sure it films down the driveway too."

"I can let you into the security office." Edgar pulled a large ring of keys from his pocket.

He and the deputy followed Edgar down the hall. "While we have the video pulled up, there's something else we need to check." As they hustled along, Trevor told them about the suspicious light and car around one a.m.

When the three men returned to the group huddled by the door, they explained what they'd seen. A video feed showed Blessie heading down the driveway around eleven fifteen. Deputy Jones decided they'd work in pairs. Additional squad cars were being dispatched. An alert would be sent out after an hour if she didn't turn up. Mrs. Paulson and Alma would coordinate the volunteers helping with the program and get the audience seated for the show. They'd change up the order to buy some time, keeping the situation quiet for now. Tammi and Edgar would remain in the foyer in case Blessie turned up.

## 11

*T*he sooner they got out there the sooner they'd find her. Trevor open and shut his hands. Could they just get moving? The group streamed out of the Center. Jones and his partner took the north route on the main road to check out the little grocers. Mark and Anna would head south and double-check the road to their house. He and Olivia were assigned to circle the new development and check the road behind the center.

Acid moved up his throat, every muscle in his body tense. "Let's go." He spotted Olivia's foot brace. "Wait, let me pull up." He pulled over, hopped out and held her elbow as she climbed in. He grabbed his dog and slid into the driver's seat, adrenaline buzzing through him. "You mind holding her? I can drive faster if she's not in my lap. There's a blanket on the floor."

She covered her knees with the blanket. The terrier hopped on.

"We *will* find Blessie. You keep track of any texts that come in." He set his jaw. They pulled down the drive and covered the access road.

Her phone pinged. "She's not by the little grocers."

They wound through the roads behind the center then back to the main road.

She shook her head, lips in a grim line. "Mark and Anna got home and are turning around. They didn't see her anywhere."

The terrier panted and whined, picking up on the mood.

"They'll get the mounted sheriff here if we don't find her soon." After circling behind the center, he pulled into the new construction area. Water stood in the recently paved streets. Dirt, soggy paper, and other construction debris that had blown around from the storm littered the area. Most of the ground was sandy mud, and tracks would easily show if anyone had walked through after the rain.

"I can't think why she'd be here," he commented, idling down the roads. They peered in the narrow spaces between the buildings, checked the stud-covered and drenched concrete slabs. No sign of Blessie. "Nobody lives here. It should be easy to see if anyone's walking around. If we see something, I'll get out. You stay in the truck."

She nodded, her face pale and tight.

Olivia wasn't looking too good. *Is she gonna have a meltdown?* If he could get her talking, she might calm. "What's going on with your foot? I've noticed you limping. Today you're wearing this brace."

"I broke my ankle this fall. It's been acting up."

He arched a brow. "The fracture's all healed?" He'd had a couple of sprains playing ball. "It's a hell of a thing, not being able to walk easily."

She told him about the injury, the difficulty healing, the ultrasound machine she used and segued into a story about her recent divorce. Then she apologized. "I'm sorry. I'm worried and... babbling."

Silence filled the car. He should say something. From the corner of his eye, he spotted a few tears on her cheek. So much for trying to make her feel better. He understood the pain of betrayal and rejection and didn't wish it on anyone. That cheating bastard had walked away from her, with an injury—unable to even get around? He shook his head, his lips curling. *What a louse.* Finally, he spoke. "That's a shame about your foot. And your ex-husband sounds like a real jerk."

She turned her face to the open window. The breeze caught her hair. When she turned back, his breath caught. She was a wild-haired beauty, cheeks pink from the cold.

He brushed aside the urge to give her the hug she needed. No time for that. Blessie was the priority. At the stop sign he briefly rubbed the back of her shoulder. "I can tell you from experience, it'll get better." He meant for his touch to be a comforting gesture, the kind he gave his students. With Olivia it was different. He wanted to put his hand back and draw her close. Divorced, beautiful, and vulnerable—oh, for the love of Pete, he was attracted to her, strongly. Not that it mattered, especially now. They had a job to do.

"This doesn't make sense." She pushed the hair out of her face.

He turned south. "You said it."

"Blessie wouldn't go wandering. She'd never get in a car with a stranger. I can't imagine her walking to Anna's house. Jones checked by the grocery. There's nothing for a couple of miles except for the railroad tracks and the garden store."

"That's it. Mark and I were discussing the garden store in front of her yesterday. I was concerned she might've heard us."

"Mark said Blessie was upset you could be getting a job there."

"I was afraid of that." He slammed the accelerator and white-knuckled the steering wheel. The Jeep bumped over the tracks.

Trevor pulled into the garden store lot, the deputy's cruiser right behind him. His gut tensed. He threw it into park and jumped out, leaving his door open.

Jones spoke sharply. "We're here to investigate the alarm. There's been a number of burglaries in the area. Wait in your vehicle." The deputy and his partner crept up to the building and began checking the doors and windows.

Trevor took a few steps toward his Jeep but needed to do something. He scanned the area. Someone ran up to the fence at the far end of the store and start shaking it. The commotion alerted Molly who pulled out of Olivia's hand and tore over to the gate.

"Mr. Weston, Mr. Weston, is that you?"

In swift strides, he moved to the chain link door

Jones yelled, "Hey, stand back."

*Not on your life.* Relief washed through him. "It's her." He wrapped his fingers through the metal links above Blessie's. "It'll be okay. We'll get you out of there."

Jones called it in. Blessie had triggered the alarm shaking the chain link door.

"Mr. Weston." She looked up with red-rimmed eyes. "I was looking for you. Let me out."

He cringed, spotting the smear of red on her hands and blood forming along small cuts on her fingers gripping the rough metal. "Are you hurt? What happened to your knee?" The torn, soiled fabric hung loose. He bent down and grabbed the dog's leash. The terrier stood on her hind legs, sticking her muzzle through the fence links.

Olivia joined him at the gate, whipped out her phone, and texted Anna. Another car pulled in behind the sheriffs' and a man sprung out.

Blessie stuck a finger through the metal, petting Molly's nose, the dog bringing a smile to her pink face. "I fell down. It's not bleeding anymore."

"We'll get you to the clinic. Hold on a few more minutes sweetie." Olivia wove her fingers over Blessie's.

"That's the man who locked me in." She angled her head toward the driver of the new vehicle who was talking to the deputy.

The man hurried over and introduced himself as the manager. "I never imagined someone would be in the outside area with all that rain. I called out I was closing. There weren't any cars in the lot." Pale and apologetic, he unlocked the door. "I didn't mean to lock her in. It was a terrible misunderstanding. I'm very sorry." The man freed Blessie, launched into an explanation about their insurance, and urged her to go to the hospital.

Trevor shook his head, fighting back an urge to punch the guy in the face. The man seemed more concerned about a lawsuit than Blessie's welfare.

Anna and Mark careened into the lot and jumped out of their truck. Blessie ran to Anna who pulled off her jacket, draped it around her sister's shoulders, and led her into Mark's pickup.

Statements were taken, paperwork signed. The manager gestured toward the Christmas display. "Please, take those poinsettias and wreaths. Consider them a donation to the Center."

Trevor glanced at Mark and shrugged. "Let's load 'em." He looked at Olivia and handed over the leash. "Could you hold Molly while we load the truck?"

"Molly?" Surprise dawned across her face.

In a few moments he and Mark tucked the plants securely in back of the Ram.

"Hurry," Anna called from the window. "We might be able to make it back to the Center and get her knee cleaned up before the singing starts. She still wants to be in the program."

He and Olivia climbed back into the Jeep. Her lips curled in a funny smile. "Molly? You call this dog Molly?"

He scratched his terrier behind the ear. "Yep, that's her name. She's a rescue. When I got her five years ago, she already had a name. No reason to change it. Molly seems to fit—don't you think?"

Olivia grinned at him. "Sure does. Odd that Miss Tammi failed to mention Molly was a dog when she told me you and Molly left this morning."

He puffed a wry laugh. *No, it makes perfect sense for Tammi.* The woman thrived on drama and was a wild card he tried to avoid.

Molly sat happily in Olivia's lap. He reached over to give his dog another pat, landing on Olivia's hand instead. His heart jumped. Awkward, he pulled it away and glanced at her. She didn't seem to mind.

"What a day." She grinned at him.

He pulled close to the entrance to help her out. By the time she unbuckled her seat belt, he had the door open and reached to steady her as she put weight on her foot. He held her left arm and placed his other hand along her ribs to lift her gently down. Olivia glanced up with a surprised expression and held his eyes, warm and inviting. That was enough. He bent down and brushed his lips against hers, gently. His hand stroked her hair, and he searched her face. Did he have permission to kiss her?

Her slight nod was the response he'd hoped for. He brought his hand to her cheek and moved his thumb gently across her skin, brushing her hair back, and kissed her again, like he meant it.

"Olivia —" his voice came out hoarse, "—you're beautiful." He lowered his forehead to hers, and they both let out a big sigh. "Man, it's good we found Blessie."

"That's for sure." She stepped back and regarded him with a curious smile.

"I need to put Molly away. I'll see you inside." What in the world was he doing, stealing a kiss right in front of the entrance? A bad idea, but he liked it.

"I'll save you a seat."

He watched her through the rearview mirror, Molly in his lap with her head out the window. Olivia had stopped, glanced his way and touched her fingertips to her lips. Something that felt a lot like hope bloomed in his chest.

What an idiot he'd been. Trevor quickly changed into a fresh shirt as he beat himself up over the unnecessary trauma he'd caused by being distracted that morning. She wouldn't have gone on that wild goose chase looking for him and gotten hurt. That was on him. But if Mark hadn't talked to Blessie about the garden store, she never would've headed there. Shoulda, coulda, woulda. At least she's safe now. He couldn't take all the blame.

He hiked back to the main building in an exhilarating breeze, the temperature steadily dropping. Palm fronds thrashed in the blustery wind against a cobalt sky. But his thoughts were on the woman saving him a seat, the sweet taste of her lips, her soft hair and silky top. It was stupid kissing her out front where people were coming and going, but at the moment, the need to feel his lips on hers had outweighed reason. He didn't know if it was the weather, finding Blessie, the plan he and Mavis were hatching, or kissing Olivia. A switch had flipped inside him, and he was finally awake, really living again. He'd been burned badly in the past. But today, moving toward the main building where he'd find Olivia waiting, excitement energized him.

Singers were climbing up the risers on the stage at the end of the room that served as both dining hall and auditorium. The skit had just ended. Blessie was back in time. He let out a sigh of relief, surveyed the good-sized crowd, and made out a few board members. Mrs. Paulson and Pastor Don, another ally on the board, worked the refreshment table dipping cups of punch and waved at him. Mavis sat across the room with a middle-aged couple, probably her family. Seth Smith stood at the side of the room with a few men in suits and cast him a dark glance. He met Smith's stare, schooling his face into a neutral expression. *Slimy jerk, putting in an appearance like he really cares about these people.*

He searched the audience. Toward the back was a row of chairs where Olivia sat next to Anna and Mark. The two granddaughters sat with another woman in front of them. There was an empty chair on the side of Mark and another to the left of Olivia. He grabbed the seat by Olivia. Mark raised an eyebrow and monitored him for a minute. He met Mark's gaze and glanced away, conflicted, drawn to Olivia, but Mark was his friend.

Piano chords softly came together in a delicate rendition of "Coventry Carole." The music of Christmas filled the hall. Blessie was right in front, singing her heart out. The lights dimmed, and a soloist came out for "O Holy Night." Twinkling lights along the stage created a magical, sacred atmosphere. Olivia glanced his way, and he resisted the urge to bring his arm around her.

*"Thank you,"* she mouthed and surprised him by reaching over and giving his hand a little squeeze. He took the opportunity to enfold her hand in his.

"Glad we found her," he whispered. Understatement. The sweet sensation of holding hands made him feel young. Olivia was nice to touch. Afraid of being too forward, he reluctantly let go. Her hand crept back, and she wove her fingers through his and rested it on his thigh. The edge of her lips curved up as she watched the show. Could she be enjoying this as much as he was? A warm feeling filled him. This evening might be even better than he'd imagined.

## 12

*W*as a successful Christmas Eve still possible? Anna's temple throbbed and her nerves were a wreck, but you couldn't ask for a more picture-perfect room. *Nobody would believe what a hellish day we've had.* It was tight getting ready. Mark, Blessie and Olivia all helped. Matthew and Natalie even pitched in when they arrived, despite coming off a nine-hour drive. The three granddaughters played quietly, out of the way.

Part of her wanted to say to hell with it all, but she knew the activity of creating a beautiful table would soothe her and restore normalcy. Decked out with holly garland, red bows, and groups of pine and cinnamon-scented candles glowing on side tables, she'd outdone herself decorating the house this year. She'd even trimmed two different Christmas trees. The larger tree twinkled brightly in the living room. Holiday music filtered softly through speakers.

She carried the platter of cheese to the table. "Hey, those are for later." No wonder the girls were so quiet. All three granddaughters were clustered around a plundered cookie platter, the evidence in hand and on their faces, along with guilty smiles.

"Grandma, we're hungry." Emily held up half of a tree shape.

Pixie giggled. "Very hungry." She had a partially eaten cookie in each hand.

Lindsay had the decorum to look sheepish. "Can I have another, Grandma? Please?"

"Have some cheese, instead." She fixed them each a little plate of cheese, meatballs, and carrots, tidied the lavish spread, and replenished the cookie tray. In addition to a pitcher of cider, eggnog filled a crystal punch bowl. For those who wanted something stronger, there was beer, wine, and a pitcher of rum-infused eggnog available in the kitchen, along with Jake's coffees and Tara's herbal tea.

Despite the beauty of it all, she got caught up in poignant memories. Holidays when her daughter, her parents, and her grandparents had been alive streamed through her mind. Those were her ghosts of Christmases past. Mostly, she missed Stephanie.

In the family room off the kitchen, Emily, Pixie, and Lindsay were settled in front of an animated Christmas show with Blessie. The sounds of their voices prompted a slight smile; her brood was happy together. Sadly, Brent had texted he'd be over in a couple of hours to get his two.

Where were her aunt and uncle? She checked her voicemail and her heart sunk. They wouldn't make it after all. Lu's mother, over a hundred years old, was in a facility, too frail for them to leave her. If she stabilized, they'd make it down for New Year's Eve.

She dropped to a seat, tears threatening to ruin her makeup. In the other room, Mark welcomed the first wave at the front door. Family this early, coming for drinks and finger foods then exchanging small gifts. Later, neighbors would join them for coffee and cakes.

"Need any help, Anna?" Tara swooped into the kitchen, carrying a tray of homemade dark chocolate truffles, a vision of Christmas in a sequined green top over black jeans. "Aren't you pretty in that red dress with the holiday cardigan?" Tara froze, her brow knit. "Why the long face?"

"This day's taken a toll on me." She released a breath. "I wish your parents could be here this year. They're the closest thing I have to Mom and Dad. Aunt Lydia never comes." She sat at the kitchen table and dabbed the corners of her lids with her fingertips. "I'm sorry I'm so emotional."

"No wonder. But everything turned out okay, right? I wish Mom and Dad were coming too. With the kids here, I was hoping for support from Mom. It hasn't been easy." Tara took the chair next to Anna and gave her arm a squeeze. "Maybe it's not the number of people you have to love, but the amount of love you show for the people you have." She paused. "I don't mean to minimize losing Stephanie. You know I love and appreciate you, Anna."

"Thank you."

Tara waved her hand to encompass the room. "As much as you're the decorating wiz—and don't get me wrong, we love that you go all out—the best part is being together. Even to have a gathering of this size is really wonderful."

"When did you get so wise?" Anna puffed a little laugh.

"Hey, I'm a stepmom. My heart's been tenderized from loving kids who I'm pretty sure, half the time, are trying to figure out how to get rid of me. But I'm grateful to have the kids with us. It's nice to be part of a family, even if Maya's been a real pill all day." Tara poured herself a large glass of eggnog from the pitcher on the counter. "Delicious, Anna."

"How's Maya doing now?" Anna wiped her cheeks with a tissue and watched Tara down half the glass of spiked eggnog. Then her cousin topped off her glass again. At this rate, she'd be feeling no pain in short order.

"Cynthia and Jonathan got here with the boys, and Madison brought Kayden tonight. I think she's glowing under all that boy attention. They're over by the fireplace comparing phones." Tara took a big slug of eggnog, drained her glass, and poured another.

"You know that has rum in it, don't you?"

Tara's jaw dropped. She shook her head, slowed down to

sipping the eggnog but didn't pour it out. The two women moved into the living room and almost got knocked over by the girls heading for the fudge Olivia'd made the previous night.

"Wow, Anna, you sure outdid yourself this year." Lexie uncovered her tray of sushi.

Madison wrinkled her nose. "I never considered sushi a holiday tradition."

"Isn't there the feast of the seven fishes or something like that?" Lexie popped a salmon roll in her mouth.

Anna studied her cousin. Everything seemed to roll right off Lexie. It must be a requirement if you were living with Madison. Despite them being quilting buddies, you had to have nerves of steel around Madison, who'd been extra crabby lately.

Olivia entered the room and twirled, showing off a silk-and-velvet maroon dress with a black satin neckline, a sparkly necklace, and earrings with garnet crystals.

"Wow. Olivia, you're beautiful." Lexie circled her with a warm hug. Even Cynthia approved. Anna filled with satisfied warmth. Olivia was perking up nicely, obviously benefitting from being back around family. Now the challenge was to be the good hostess, monitor her granddaughters and keep her cousin away from Trevor all at the same time. Could she enlist one of her cousins to help her keep them apart?

Olivia's heart leaped at the sound of the doorbell and dropped again when it wasn't Trevor. Had he decided not to come? He hadn't texted her, but why would he? That was supposed to be for work. Conversation was flowing and people were seated or standing in small groups near the food. She drifted down the hall into the quiet den. A nautical-themed tabletop tree was strung with blue, green, and white lights, casting an enchanting glow in the dim room. Ornaments of fish, mermaids, and shells caught the lights and sparkled. She reached out to touch a crystal starfish and was interrupted by a deep voice.

"Mind if I join you?"

*Trevor.* Butterflies fluttered in her stomach. She smelled his spicy aftershave before pivoting to the tall man behind her. "I didn't know you were here." Laughter from the other room seemed far away. The kiss they'd shared at the Center flashed across her mind and she licked her lips.

"There's a pretty one." He reached to adjust a glass ornament in the shape of a sea urchin.

A shiver ran up her arm as he brushed against her.

"I like the way it catches the light." She lifted her gaze to his, breathless. A gentleman, he was waiting for her to set the pace.

His hooded, intense gaze sought hers and held. Her smile must've been the green light he was waiting for, because he placed his fingers on the side of her cheek, lowered his face, and kissed her long and sweet, standing back several inches.

She lifted her hands to the sides of his face and traced his scratchy whiskers. "That was nice."

"How about another?" This time, his large hands spread over her back. He pulled her in and covered her lips with his.

She let go of any resistance and relaxed into his embrace, the kiss growing passionate, hungry, and making her lightheaded. "I think I need to sit down." What was she doing? The voice of reason faded. She didn't want to stop.

"Sure, let's sit here on the couch." He held her as they stepped over to the couch, sat, and he circled her with his arm. "Okay?"

She grinned and nodded. *More than okay.* Her heart was opening to this man, but her brain warned her, *hold back.* He leaned down, pulled her nearer, and crashed his mouth to hers. His free hand moved from her cheek to her hair, to her back, warm across the thin fabric.

He kissed the side of her neck. "Your hair's so soft," he whispered hoarsely, pushing a strand behind her ear and bringing his lips to hers again. *Holy moly. Heaven.* Then he pulled away and leaned back against the couch.

Gathering a breath, she turned toward the window willing her heart to calm. *We should go in the other room.* "I can't believe we're here hiding out in the den, making out like a couple of kids." She laughed softly.

"You can say that again. But..." A slow grin spread across his face as he locked hooded eyes on her. "There's plenty more where that came from." They sat in silence for a long moment. Music and laughter drifted down the hall. He reached over, and his strong fingers intertwined hers. He brought her hand to his lips and kissed her knuckles, the back of her hand, the inside of her wrist.

She shivered. How could kissing her hand feel so... intimate?

He stared at her face with his lips on her wrist. "Nice perfume." He set her hand back on the couch, keeping hold of it. "So, Olivia, tell me about yourself. I know you taught and you're an artist."

She talked. He listened. She kept her fingers laced in his calloused hand and shared as he asked questions. He seemed to care about what she said and not like he was using a well-practiced skill set. His attentive listening, kisses and kindness were capturing her heart.

"Hey everyone, it's time," Madison's voice rang out. "Come into the living room—we're opening gifts."

## 13

*T*revor reluctantly released Olivia's hand, congratulating himself on his restraint. It wasn't that he didn't want to listen to her, but she was so kissable and he wanted more of her. When they rounded the corner to look for seats, Mark caught his eye with a question on his face. He gave his friend a little nod. *He's got his eye on me.*

He hadn't planned to spend time in the den kissing Olivia. But when he'd spotted her walking in there, he'd followed his urge to be with her, telling himself they'd talk. Then she'd looked up at him. Any restraint was lost. He hadn't felt so alive in years and didn't want it to stop. Now he was torn between the crisis at work, and of all people, Olivia, Mark's family. *What in the hell am I doing? Mark's my friend.*

"Sit here, sit here, Mr. Weston." Blessie patted a place next to her at the end of the couch near the tree. He wanted to be close to Olivia but took the seat next to Blessie. At least Olivia took the chair between him and Blessie's blind cousin, Jennifer. After a moment, the kids helped a woman named Natalie pass out the gifts. There's no way he'd keep all these cousins straight so he just smiled and decided not to worry about it.

Most of the festively wrapped presents seemed to be home-made, but the teens got gift cards and the youngsters got toys. The smallest, Pixie, crunched a candy cane and kept asking if she could open her present. So much like his daughter Cherie, his throat closed up a couple of times. That was right around the size she'd been when Stacy had taken her away.

He gave Mark a new softball mitt as a thank you for helping coach the athletics. Mark and Anna gave him leather garden gloves. Then he passed around pots of basil he'd grown, glad he'd taken the time to tie them with green satin ribbon—they seemed to be a big hit.

Anna and Olivia passed out homemade sourdough bread and cranberry loaves for everyone. He could watch Olivia move around all night, more beautiful than ever in that dress. The memory of the silky fabric under his hands filtered through his mind as he followed her with his gaze. He received tins of cookies made by the little girls. Jake and his sister Tara had put together gift baskets of coffee and teas. Maybe the oddest gift was a set of little glass roller bottles holding scented oils, with labels explaining their properties. Jake's older daughter, Madison, had made them.

He'd been selling Jake produce for the café ever since Blessie had started at the Center. The café owner was a standup guy. Together they were working out how to grow coffee plants in a small greenhouse in Jake's backyard. That polished couple, Cynthia and Jonathan, handed out small Swarovski crystal figurines, trees and reindeer. Anna chided her for going way outside the recom-mended limit for spending on gifts. Tender feelings came over him as he dragged his thumb over the cranberry loaf, took in the garden gloves, and studied the miniature crystal tree. He hadn't expected to receive gifts.

When the commotion settled, he ducked around to where he'd left flowers stashed in a box. He gave a vase of yellow-green St. Patrick's roses to Anna, pleased with her obvious delight. Then he surprised Olivia with a crystal vase of Veteran's Honor tea roses, ruby-red with a sweet fragrance. He thanked her for stepping up to help in the art room—at least, that's the excuse he'd given himself when he'd cut her a bunch of flowers.

Color crept into her cheeks when she accepted them. "I'm sorry I don't have more for you." She nodded at the loaves.

"No worries." He shrugged, warmth filling his chest, wanting to reach out and move his hand over her soft olive skin, push her hair back and kiss those full lips. For crying out loud, he was falling for her. So soon? How was that even possible? More importantly, did he have time for this while he was working to straighten out his job? Distraction had already proved disastrous earlier that day. Didn't the good of the Center and all the residents come first?

Olivia buried her nose in the soft petals of the roses. Yes, he'd said it was a thank you, but it seemed like such a romantic gesture and reminded her of his kisses less than an hour earlier. Over the top of the bouquet, Cynthia squinted in her direction. She could practically hear the gears in her sister's mind working, and it wouldn't be good. But she couldn't avoid Cynthia all night.

Seated next to Olivia, Jennifer ran her fingers over the basil leaves and inhaled. "Don't you love the fragrance of the basil?" Next, she lifted the cranberry bread to her face. "Mm, this smells divine. I can't wait to try it, Olivia."

As the gifts were passed around, Olivia described the proceedings to her blind cousin. Maya opened a gift card from Anna; Pixie was squealing over a little art set.

"Olivia, I don't know if you get how glad I am you're back." Jennifer leaned closer. "Anna told me she invited you to stay here with them instead of going out to Texas. I'd like that. I've missed you."

"I'm really glad to be here too, but I'm not sure how long I'm staying. The woman at the Center says they could use my help through January, so possibly until then. I'm not sure what to do. I need to save some money. I'm pretty broke." She listened to Jennifer but watched Trevor, who was chatting amiably with Blessie.

"I appreciate having another artist here," Jennifer continued, oblivious to her interest in Trevor.

If she moved back, the current of helping others would sweep her up. Olivia studied Blessie. If she stayed, she'd be running her cousin around, checking on her at the Center and getting involved in activities with Anna. It was wonderful to live with them while she'd finished high school, and she'd always be grateful for that. But if she moved back in, Anna'd probably try to micromanage her life like in the past. Could she stand up for herself if she came back to live?

Trevor was laughing with Blessie. He was a good man. How he would fit into her life if she chose to remain in town? Would it be awkward? She was drawn to him and wanted to explore that possibility.

Jennifer was still talking. "Madison and Anna quilt together. Lexie sometimes comes over to throw pots at the studio, but she's just learning. You're already good at ceramics."

"I'd love to get back into clay." Olivia turned her attention back to Jennifer.

"You know, when you were in high school and you did clay with me, that was what got me into it in the first place. Then Nanny took over when you left and look at me now. The clay studio might not even exist if you hadn't had the time and patience to show me how to roll coils and make those first pinch pots." Jennifer leaned closer. "Actually, if you stay here, I have a little proposition for you."

An ambush was the last thing she'd expected when Olivia walked into the kitchen to find plates and utensils for the cake. Hadn't she and Trevor been discreet?

"Hey Olivia, it looks like you got something special for Christmas." Lexie poured herself a large, spiked eggnog and cut her a mischievous glance.

"What?" She feigned innocence and busied herself with the plates, her pulse picking up as though she were guilty of something.

Lexie grinned. "Those roses. And I saw you in the den with Trevor."

In waltzed her sister, face drawn into a severe frown. "Have fun with him but keep it casual. Don't go falling for this guy." Cynthia folded her arms and tapped a beautifully manicured finger on her crimson lips. "He looks like he's good for a fling or a transition man."

"Transition?" Olivia tilted her head. Was her sister for real?

"Yes, you know, the handsome guy you date after your divorce. Lots of my friends have a little fun with guys like that between husbands. He's not the type you want to settle down with. What does he do? Shovel stables? Work in a garden? A teacher? Don't fall for this guy. He doesn't have much to offer you."

She furrowed her brow and studied the tile floor. *Bite your tongue, it's Christmas.*

Cynthia wouldn't let up. "He works at the Center? You can do better. Besides, you really should come out to Dallas. Jonathan has lots of business associates. Phillip does too. I'm sure we can set you up with someone who's more appropriate. You have this disability with your foot. You need someone who can take care of you, Olivia." Her sister gave her a tight smile.

She chewed her lip, so angry she could spit. Immature as it was, Cynthia saying she should move to Dallas made her not want to go. Her sister didn't have a clue about her life or what she wanted. "I don't know what you're talking about with 'transition' man. And if I decide to date this guy, that's my life. I'm teaching art part time at the Center next week and he helped me get the job. And Anna and Mark said I'm welcome to stay here until I get on my feet."

"And after everything they've been through with Stephanie and Blessie, don't you think they need a break?" Cynthia's lips pressed into a thin line and she tilted her head. "You're working at the Center with all those disabled people?" Her sister released an exasperated sigh. "Okay, honey, I'm simply trying to help. Like you said, it's your life." She raised her palms, turned, and clicked her way back to Jonathan.

Tara stepped forward, a little unsteady. *Has she been drinking? She never drinks.*

"Olivia, don't get upset." Tara grabbed her arm. "But this time, Cynthia might be right. Trevor's nice, but Jake says he doesn't date. I'm sure there's someone with less baggage out there. Jake told me Trevor has an ex-wife and a daughter who live up north somewhere. I don't know if he's still stuck on her or what."

"Can I please get you some coffee?" Olivia huffed. Tara had been her confidant through the problems with Steele and was being over-protective.

Jennifer moved into the kitchen, trailing along the wall with her hand. She stepped over to the group. "Is this where everyone is?"

"Hey, Jen. We're discussing Olivia's love life and deciding if Trevor is right for her." Lexie took her niece's arm and guided her alongside the counter.

"More like my lack of a love life."

Jennifer's tone perked up. "Olivia, you like Trevor? He seems like a great person. He delivers produce to the café and is always super nice to me. And he's helping dad with his coffee plants."

"You have my permission to enjoy him and have fun." Lexie gave her a wicked grin.

Tara winced, weaving toward her younger sister. "You would say that Lexie. You're all about fun. But Olivia doesn't need to get her heart broken again so soon."

"Stop it. I'm not getting my heart broken." Why were they all over her? "It was only a kiss. And I agree with Jennifer. He seems like a great guy." She'd loved it when he'd held her in his arms and would like the chance to get used to that. But she wasn't telling her cousins.

"Hey, where are those plates?" Madison called. "We've got the cakes cut."

Ribbons, bows, and holiday paper strewn across the floor were gathered in the nick of time before the doorbell rang. In walked two sets of neighbors. Introductions were made, coffee was poured, and for a moment the room hushed as people were eating. Then everyone began talking at once, comparing the different varieties of cakes baked this year. Tara voted for the new addition, carrot cake. The little girls and Blessie all voted the candy cane cake as the winner. Laughter and moans from being too full filled the room.

"Ladies, you outdid yourself again." Mark patted his stomach.

Olivia nibbled on the banana cake but the butterflies in her stomach reduced her appetite. Trevor sampled carrot cake, banana cake, and a little piece of the candy cane cake to please Blessie.

She collected the empty plates and wove her way into the kitchen toward the sink. It touched her to see how good he was with her cousin. If she stayed, perhaps he'd be that good to her.

## 14

The evening was going by too fast and now she had to get through saying goodbye to their granddaughters. Anna helped Brent round up the girls while his fiancée waited in the car. "Are you sure you two can't come in and stay a while?" She hated to see them leave. Emily circled her waist with her little arms. She bent down for hugs, breathing in the scent of baby shampoo and kissed her granddaughters goodbye. *You will not break down.* She tensed her face and forced a smile.

Brent, who'd been like a son to her, offered thanks and hugged her. He grabbed one large tote filled with gifts and another filled with baked goods, half of the candy cane cake, and walked to the car, Rena was already strapping the girls into their car seats.

Anna bit her lip and watched Mark carry the girls' suitcases to the car. He may as well have ripped out her heart and shut it in the trunk with their bags. Tears rimmed her lids as she waved goodbye. Mark took her by the arm and pulled her in for a big hug. They stood on the front porch and held one another, soothed by the bracing cold. Under the pretty lights covering the entrance to her home, she took a jagged breath.

"You okay?" whispered Mark as he kissed her forehead.

She shook her head. "I'll never be okay. But I'll adjust. Are you?"

Mark kept his feelings locked in a vault. He gave a quick nod. A flash of pain worked over his face, gone as fast as it appeared. Anna watched him tighten into his brave smile, and they joined the others inside the house.

~~~~~

What was taking Olivia so long? Trevor surveyed the room, over the top with holiday cheer, candles, and figurines on every surface. Anna could open her own shop. He chuckled to himself, but there was something comforting about being enfolded in the festive sense of Christmas she created.

Jake took the chair next to him. "You need to come by and check out the plants. They're coming up and looking good." The café owner didn't just want to roast his own beans, he wanted to grow them too. He'd helped the guy build a greenhouse and they were experimenting with humidity and temperature options, since coffee plants didn't typically grow at sea level in Florida and the native version, Psychotria nervosa, didn't produce as flavorful beans. After a while Jake left to check on his blind daughter.

To his left he registered Mark shutting the front door. The woman with red curls cornered him. Whatever she said, his buddy wasn't taking it well. Mark's expression changed from concerned to looking downright pissed.

A grey striped cat appeared out of nowhere and leaped into his lap. "Well, hello there." Growing up, he'd always had cats and dogs, but when he'd adopted Molly from the rescue, they'd warned him she didn't get along with cats. He took advantage of the situation and ran his hand down the cat's back and along its tail, then scratched the side of his face. It purred and kneaded his shirt.

Olivia returned, holding two steaming mugs and her eyes popped wide. "Tiger likes you? Watch out, he scratches and bites. I thought Anna locked him up."

"He seems fine so far."

She held out his coffee, the scent of cinnamon and nutmeg wafted over. "Jake's holiday blend, cream, no sugar, right?"

"You pay attention." He reached for the cup, touched she'd cared enough to remember how he'd taken his coffee earlier, and gestured toward the space remaining on the couch.

She squeezed in, lighting a fire along his leg where she pressed against him. He could move over to give her more space, but then wouldn't be able to enjoy the closeness of her. Tiger curled up and went to sleep on his lap. "I'd move over but I can't disturb..." He gestured at Tiger and lifted the edge of his mouth in a tease.

"No. We can't disturb the cat." She flashed a flirty smile.

On the television across the room, the 1938 version of *A Christmas Carol* played with closed captions. They sat in companionable silence for a few minutes while he was keenly aware Olivia's lavender scent and soft presence. *I could get used to her next to me.*

Now that she had that temp job, he could get to know her. Could be he was reading something into it, but the way she looked at him, the way she kissed him, felt like an invitation. Should he discuss his intentions regarding Olivia with his friend? Was that old-fashioned? It seemed reasonable. What were his intentions? Undeniable attraction, deep, strong. She tugged at his heart too, he took note of how kind she was to Blessie and Jennifer and how good she was with the girls.

Blessie had told him Olivia'd lived with Mark and Anna back in high school. He didn't want to damage a friendship by messing around with someone who was like a daughter to his buddy. It made sense to wait until after the whole business with the board was settled. No sense jumping the gun. If he lost his job, he wasn't sure he'd even stay in town.

By nine thirty, most of the people had gone home. Olivia took his hand and led him outdoors. "Come and see how the dock is decorated."

He slipped his arm around her. "Is it too cold for you?"

"It's just right for Christmas. I'm good."

They crossed the backyard to the dock, strewn with colorful lights, and stood over the creek. The neighbors in both directions had also put up decorations, and the effect of all the little lights reflecting in the water silenced them. The tide lapping on the pilings combined with the salty odor of the brackish water and bright stars in the clear winter sky. "This is…"

"I know." She looked up and smiled.

He lowered his mouth to hers, and they stood linked together. She parted her lips, and he lost himself in kissing this tempting, beautiful woman. Then, he stood for a long moment simply holding her close to him. After a few minutes he tore himself away, and they walked around the house toward his Jeep, holding hands. When they reached his car, he circled her with his arms and sandwiched himself between her and the car, taking the cold on his own back. Her arms circled his ribs beneath his jacket. He pulled her into his chest and rested his chin on the top of her hair, breathing in the scent she wore. He hated to leave. How could he extend his time with her? "Hey, how do you like the beach when it's cold out?"

"I haven't been to the beach in the winter in years."

"I know it's Christmas tomorrow, but could you get away for a little while? How about in the afternoon? I'm working part of the day. I volunteered to help cover the dining room in the morning. A lot of staff wanted off for the holiday."

"Yes, that could work."

The lights behind her framed her face giving her an angelic glow. He could look at her all night. "Good." He brought his lips to her forehead.

"We have dinner later, but nothing in the middle of the day."

"How about I pick you up, close to one, and we ride out to the beach for a while?" He held the side of her face and stole one more kiss before climbing in his car.

Unfamiliar lightness filled him as he aimed his Jeep toward the

Center and drove into the night. Olivia sparked a possibility he'd long ago abandoned. He sang along with his Country Christmas playlist and kept on singing as he entered his cottage.

This had been the best Christmas Eve in years. For starters, he hadn't spent it alone. Sure, folks remained at Sacred Haven for the holiday. He'd spent many a Christmas Eve playing checkers with residents before hunkering down with Molly in an empty cottage to watch TV. But tonight, it was as though he'd been with family, and there was Olivia—he warmed at the memory of her. She'd explained about her students, her art, and quilt making. And she'd beamed when she told him how she'd volunteered in the program for teen mothers, teaching them to quilt blankets for their babies. Clearly, she really cared about making a difference in those girls' lives. Plus, she'd taken the art position to help out at the Center; that meant something too. Yep, in addition to being beautiful, she seemed to be a good person.

But his nerves broadcasted a warning. Why let himself get all sentimental? It was attraction and the lonely holiday. *Get a grip.* He'd tried a relationship, had been married before. All he had to show for it was a stomped heart and years of child support payments for a daughter he'd hardly gotten to see. Never once had he forgotten her birthday—he'd gotten no acknowledgement whatsoever. He'd surrendered to the fact that she had enough family without him.

He rubbed the bridge of his nose and groaned, the old pain was back that quickly. His daughter had never needed him. The fact stung. A walk outside would clear his head. He grabbed Molly's leash and took her into the cold night. Every time he dug up those old memories, he got so pissed. Why did he do that to himself?

It was officially Christmas, ten after midnight, when he opened the door to the warm cottage. Despite his misgivings, he'd give Olivia a chance. She wasn't Stacy, nothing like her. Tomorrow afternoon, he'd take her to the beach.

In the morning, he'd help serve breakfast. He knew the drill.

Each resident would have a stocking with gifts and treats waiting at their place at the table, courtesy of a local church. After clearing the breakfast, they'd go to the community room for carols. Gifts from the angel tree would be passed out, things they weren't able to get for themselves, electronic devices, clothes. It wasn't a bad way to spend Christmas morning. But it wasn't his idea of the ideal holiday.

Wouldn't it be nice to spend Christmas with a wife and family of his own? He allowed himself to dream. They'd share a quiet cup of coffee and sit near the tree together. Like tonight with Olivia. It sure had been nice kissing her by that tree in the den.

Before turning in, he did a quick email check. Right at the top was a message from Cherie. *Cherie's in Naples with her boyfriend? She wants to drive up tomorrow afternoon for a visit?* His heart did a little flip. He dashed off a reply. *Of course, come.* If she'd known she was coming to Florida, why hadn't she made arrangements to see him earlier? He shook his head. It didn't matter. If his baby girl wanted to come up for a visit on Christmas, that'd be the best gift he could imagine. "Woo-hoo! Molly girl, Cherie's coming."

The sleepy-eyed terrier cocked her head and yawned before dropping it back on her bed.

He shucked his clothes, climbed into bed, and couldn't stop smiling. His girl was coming on Christmas. And on top of that, there was a woman he actually enjoyed seeing— Olivia.

Uh-oh. Olivia. He'd made plans with her for tomorrow afternoon. They were only riding out to the beach for a couple of hours. It shouldn't be a problem to bump it over to Sunday. He reached for his phone. Too late to call. What to write? He dashed off a text. *Need to move the beach to Sunday afternoon. Something's come up. Talk later.*

Should he text about Cherie coming? He hadn't even told Olivia about his daughter. His situation was too complicated to explain in a text. He'd give her a more detailed account when he saw her on Sunday. Surrounded by so much family, she'd be okay with the change.

## 15

*H*appier than she'd been in recent memory, Olivia inhaled the sweet scent of the red roses she'd placed on the table next to her bed. Spun-sugar cirrus clouds curved in the blue Christmas morning sky, and small patches of frost glistened on the rooftops. There was still enough time before breakfast to slip into the garage and dig around in the bin of her art quilts.

The one with a watermelon theme would be perfect for Trevor. A big deal, he'd likely recognize how much time the quilt took to make. She brought it in and wrapped it. Her mouth went dry with excitement and she paused, holding the soft wrapped package to her chest. Was this the message she wanted to send? Possibly this was too much too soon.

Trevor had waved off the roses, saying they covered his bushes right now. Still, when he'd handed them to her, she swore she'd seen something in his expression. Was she reading too much into it? When he'd kissed her in front of that tree, it'd been like a scene right out of a movie. For once, she'd played the heroine, like Sleeping Beauty when the prince kissed her. Part of her had been sleeping, more like in a coma. He woke her up.

She touched her shoulder, remembering how he'd pulled her

over. Then they'd gone back to join the others like nothing had happened. But something inside her had shifted. She'd thought they'd played it so cool. Nobody would notice the flush in her cheeks. Wrong! Had she ever gotten ambushed when she'd gone in the kitchen.

Thank goodness Madison hadn't come into the kitchen and helped with the ambush. She would've raised objections based on the fact that Trevor was Blessie's teacher. Her cousin may be right. Would seeing Trevor be a risk to both her and Blessie? Was she being selfish? Keep things superficial, a little handholding, an occasional kiss, a dinner, then break away—that was what she ought to do.

She'd perfected making a mess out of her life. It was time for a change. Wasn't that what becoming Olivia 2.0 meant? This morning's reading in her little book had said "Anything is possible." Appropriate for Christmas, a time to think about miracles. Anything's possible—right? It'd be a miracle if she got a good job right away. And it'd take a miracle for her and Trevor to amount to anything. But the time they'd spent together had been so sweet. They'd only just met, but they weren't kids anymore.

Conflicted and torn, her head was beginning to throb. How'd it make sense to get involved when everything was in flux? It didn't. So why'd she want to give him the quilt?

The savory aroma of eggs and bacon and apple-cinnamon called Olivia into the kitchen where Mark, Matthew, and Blessie sat at the table set with poinsettia-rimmed plates. Lindsay sipped her juice as Anna dished up the crumbly cake. Matthew smiled at her through half-closed lids and barely held his head up. "More coffee?" She raised the pot in his direction and gave him a refill before getting her own.

"Look what Santa brought me." Lindsay lifted a stuffed giraffe.

"We let her open one Santa gift before breakfast." Natalie planted a kiss on her daughter's head. "The rest are for after you eat. And I noticed a stocking for everyone."

Olivia glanced at Anna with a smile of appreciation. *Mrs. Claus* had made everyone a bulging stocking filled with treats and little gifts. She couldn't remember the last time she'd had an actual Christmas stocking to open.

"How's your foot today?" asked Mark as he dished strawberries onto Lindsay's plate.

"I'm actually really good today. Stronger, you know?" Barely hiding her excitement as she spoke to Mark, she continued. "I may put my brace on for the beach with Trevor this afternoon. But I feel great now."

Mark studied her a moment, his brows lowering as if concerned. "I'm sure you'll have a great time."

"I'll go with you," Blessie chimed in.

"No. You're coming to church with us, aren't you?" Anna put the strata on the table.

Blessie raised her shoulders. "Okay."

"It's only because it's Christmas that Matthew's up. He was so wired last night from driving in that traffic, he didn't sleep." Natalie tousled her husband's dark hair. He smiled up at her, took her hand, and kissed the back of her fingers, the love between them palpable.

Olivia studied them with longing. They were lucky. The warm feelings for her family weren't enough. She craved what Matthew and Natalie had. Would she ever find it?

They took their coffees into the living room and Anna put on instrumental holiday music. A frenzy of opening stockings and gifts followed. Olivia gave everyone quilted wall hangings: blue herons for Anna and Mark, and one with pink spoonbills for Blessie. The one for Natalie and Matthew was appliquéd with orange and red peaches—corny, since they lived in Georgia, but really pretty. Blessie gave everyone potholders she'd woven herself. Lindsay jumped up and down when she unwrapped the large old-fashioned doll house with little dolls.

Anna gave her peridot earrings and had sewn her a jacket in forest green, and Mark had put a note in the card. "Forget about the cost of the tire. It's part of your gift." She hugged Anna and kissed Mark's cheek, her heart brimming with gratitude. They were so good to her.

Tiger chased the ribbons as the women gathered discarded tissue and scraps of wrapping paper. Olivia laughed and shooed the cat away.

"Didn't I see you with a big package?" Anna glanced toward the conspicuous gift sitting on the chair by the door.

"Yes. I got one of my quilts to give Trevor this afternoon."

Anna's head snapped around, her gaze narrow and an unsettling sensation gripped Olivia.

Natalie lifted her palms. "I don't know, Livy. He cuts a few flowers, so you give him something that took weeks to put together? Maybe you should give it to me."

"Do you think it's too much?" Olivia carried the mugs to the kitchen.

"It was a lot of work. It might be..." Anna paused a long moment. "I understand Trevor doesn't have any family around and he'd probably love receiving such a nice gift. Still, it's too much, sweetie. After all, what kind of message would it send?"

That wasn't the response she'd wanted. Why argue? Usually she'd take her older cousin's advice. But it was time for her to think for herself, and she might want to send a message.

After watching her cousins drive off to church, Olivia worked off her happy energy cleaning up while Matthew headed back to bed for a nap. The silence filling the house was a welcome contrast to the commotion of the morning. Had Trevor called it a date? She couldn't remember, but picking out an outfit and fixing her hair, she decided it qualified as one. A soft tunic sweater over leggings would do. It'd be cold on the beach with the sea breeze. She took extra time with her makeup, then unplugged her phone from the charger. *What's this?* A text from Trevor? He needed to bump their trip to the beach to tomorrow afternoon. Deflated, she sat on the edge of the bed, surprised by the sinking feeling in her belly. *Why didn't I check earlier?* No voicemail.

Trevor hadn't given much in the way of an explanation. Something'd come up. *On Christmas?* Last night he'd said he was helping with the Christmas morning festivities at the Center. Did he have to work all day? *Darn.* She'd looked forward to spending the afternoon with him.

She took a deep breath and allowed the wave of sadness to move through her. Outside, she noticed drips beat a slow rhythm off the roof. She cracked a window and gulped the cold air.

Now the afternoon stretched out long and lonely. The house felt deserted. She wandered from room to room, looking at the decorations, unable to enjoy their charm. What was Steele doing this morning? *Don't go there.* How could she even think of him? Maybe she'd start reading the notebook she picked up at the Center. She needed to review it at some point. But on Christmas?

Brainstorm. What if she drove to the Center and dropped off the gift? Not as good as giving it to him in person, but it might be a nice surprise when he got back from whatever he had to do. Whatever he was doing must be pretty important for him to cancel on Christmas Day. She grabbed her keys, scribbled Matthew a note, and with the package under her arm, hopped in the car.

≈≈≈

Cheerful Christmas decorations covered Sacred Haven from one end to the other. Hundreds of outdoor lights, an angel display, sparkling spiral trees, and a brightly lit reindeer welcomed visitors as they approached the entrance. Buoyed by her clever idea, Olivia practically pranced through the chilly parking lot into the building. The double doors hissed open, and she stood next to a tall Christmas tree in the foyer, hugging her festively wrapped package. The aroma of sweet baked goods wafted down the hall. Music, laughter, and voices came from the direction of the community room. Lunchtime near, she spotted the tables set in the dining room. Through the other set of double doors leading to the grounds behind the main building, two stucco cottages sat along the fence near a slash pine forest. Trevor's jeep was parked in one of the driveways. He must be here working.

"Can I help you, dear?" Mrs. Paulson seemed to appear out of nowhere. "Are you looking for someone?"

"Is Trevor Weston available?" Her face heated to be holding such a conspicuously large, wrapped gift. "I have something to drop off. I wasn't sure if he's working."

Mrs. Paulson rolled her lips into a line. "He left clear instructions not to disturb him this afternoon." Her stern expression told Olivia there was nothing more. The woman, dressed like a grandmother in a soft holiday cardigan, sounded more like a warden. Then she added, with more gentleness in her voice, "The man rarely takes time off. When he asks not to be disturbed, we don't disturb him. I have to respect that."

She swallowed hard, attempting to keep a neutral expression. What should she do? This woman wasn't letting her pass.

As though reading her mind, the dorm parent added, "Would you like to leave the package in the office? It should be safe there. It's locked, and I'll make sure he knows about it. Come along this way. Let's put it where he can get it later." She turned and made quick progress down the hall.

Olivia hustled to keep up, wavering in her decision. Perhaps this wasn't her best idea. She wouldn't get to see him open it, but everyone liked a Christmas surprise, right?

Mrs. Paulson unlocked the office. Along the wall was a bank of mailboxes. Trevor's was on the end. "If you put it in that chair—" the woman pointed to a spot beside the mailboxes, "—I'm sure he'll see it next time he comes up. And I'll mention it to him, dear." She gave a curt nod. "If there's nothing else I can do for you, I need to get back to the community room." They stepped into the hall, and the older woman locked the office. "See? All safe. Merry Christmas." Mrs. Paulson strode back down the hall.

Olivia walked to the quiet foyer and took a seat in the chair next to the tree, bothered. In her excitement, she'd forgotten a card. There was only a gift tag. What would she write in a card to Trevor?

Movement out back caught her eye. She stood and peered through the rear double doors, across the grounds. A sporty black Mercedes had pulled in and parked alongside Trevor's Jeep. Long, graceful legs ending in red heels swung out of the driver's door. A thin woman with sleek black hair and a fitted red dress with a matching little jacket emerged. She walked toward the cottage on the right. A moment later, Trevor stepped out of the front door. The woman approached him and walked right into his open arms. Joy was written across Trevor's face. He put his arm around her, and they disappeared in his cottage.

Olivia's heart jumped. Her fingertips became icy. What's going on? When she'd been confused about Molly that had been a misunderstanding, initiated by Tammi. Molly was a dog. There was no mistaking this was a woman. A beautiful, chic-looking woman. And in Trevor's arms.

Her cheeks burned. How homespun was she, standing here, wearing leggings, a long sweater, and worn tennis shoes? Definitely not couture. How naïve. She had to get the quilt and take it back home. She stormed to the office and tried the door. Of course, it was locked, she'd seen Mrs. Paulson lock it. What was it with locked doors in this place? She could ask the woman to unlock the office. No. She couldn't face her in her current state. Was she a fool or what? Trevor had blown her off for the skinny woman with the silky black hair.

Pounding charged in her chest. She couldn't take back the quilt now. What would he read into this? *Exactly what you wanted him to. But evidently, he doesn't feel the same way.* Mark said he didn't think Trevor had a girlfriend, but that didn't mean he didn't have women he casually dated. Oh, good grief. That woman was much younger, thinner, and dressed so elegantly. What did that say about him?

Despite the way he'd kissed, she probably wasn't even his type. All the pain she'd experienced with Steele came rushing to the surface. She turned and limped out to her car as fast as her aching foot would take her, blinking back hot tears of humiliation.

As she sped away from the center, she attempted to untangle her feelings. Yes, she was thrilled he'd given her flowers, but they were from his garden. It took nothing to do that. He'd given Anna flowers too. Trevor was a flirt. The others were right. She's out of practice dating and would get her heart broken. Why had she thrown herself at this man she'd just met? Of course her instincts were off. Look at the bad behavior she'd tolerated from Steele. She scurried home into the comfort of her dark guest room and pulled the covers over her head.

## 16

*B*est Christmas ever. Trevor couldn't get enough of Cherie's beautiful face. She slipped out of her cropped red cashmere jacket and gave him a shy grin. Was she nervous?

"I can see you're still embracing minimalism, Dad." She plopped into the leather chair near the window. "I remember being here, what, twelve years ago? It seems pretty much the same. Is that sofa different from the pull-out you slept on to give me the bedroom?"

"Got it a few years ago. Let me make you something to drink, and you can tell me how I got so lucky to have you here today." He nodded toward the counter, laden with gifts from the Christmas Eve gathering. "I have all kinds of teas and coffees, cookies, and loaves of bread."

"I noticed. Coffee's good. What's up with that? Are you opening your own café?"

He chuckled. "The family I was with last night is big on beverages and baking." An image of the pleasant evening flashed through his mind and landed on Olivia. He brushed it away to focus on his beautiful baby girl right in his living room. And she wasn't a baby girl anymore. She'd grown into a beautiful young woman, who thankfully resembled his side more than her mother. "What's with the black hair, sweetie? Your natural color is so pretty."

"Just mixing it up, Dad."

He French pressed a couple mugs of holiday blend, held up the cream, and she nodded. He brought her the mug, kept one for himself, and sat opposite her on the sofa. "I've got to admit, honey, it's a surprise to have you here. A really nice surprise. What's going on?"

"Mom was in an accident a little over a week ago."

His pulse quickened. "Is she..."

"She's okay now. But they kept her in the hospital a few nights. So Ray sent me to the house to pack a bag for her." Wrinkles gathered across her forehead, and her tone developed an edge. "While I was searching through the closet looking for her slippers, I knocked down a box. It opened, and a stack of cards and letters fell out." She met his gaze, her chin wobbled. "From you, Dad. They were all from you."

His jaw tightened. That explained a few things. He kept his wrath in check as she continued.

"Of course, I read them. I was so angry. I wanted to storm into the hospital room and confront Mom, but Jared convinced me to wait until she was stronger."

He nodded slowly and waited.

"You didn't stop loving me."

His jaw dropped, incredulous. "Are you serious? I sent you email too. Baby girl, I'd never..."

She moved to the couch.

He squeezed her in his arms. "I'll always love you, and..." He rubbed his hand over her back. "You're too thin, sweetie."

"Dad." She gave him a pained look. "Anyway, we were coming down to spend the holiday with Jared's folks in Naples, and I wanted to surprise you."

"Mission accomplished." He was still reeling from the notion she could think he didn't love her.

"And ask you to walk me down the aisle when Jared and I get married in June."

His heart leaped. "That'd make me very happy. When do I get to meet the lucky guy who gets to marry my girl?"

How could he catch up with a daughter he hadn't seen in over ten years, now more woman than child? He gave her the grand tour of the grounds, the greenhouse, and the new rose garden. She fed carrot slices to the horses and picked a huge bouquet of roses to take back to Jared's folks.

He wanted her to have a special gift, pulled a small volume of poetry off his shelf and pressed it into her hands. "This belonged to your great-grandma Paula. She wrote one of the poems." He opened to the table of contents and showed her.

"I barely remember her. Are you sure you want to part with this? I know how close you were." She clutched the book to her heart and kissed his cheek.

The remainder of the afternoon, they sat on his sofa and indulged in the plate of cookies and the cranberry bread. Molly did her best to cover Cherie with dog kisses. She laughed, cried, raged at her mom, filled him in on her life, told him about meeting her fiancée. She was finishing a bachelor's degree in animal biology and applying to graduate programs.

"I'm looking at Florida. There's a good veterinary college. Jared's a website designer and can work from anywhere and even said he wouldn't mind moving. After all, his parents are down here."

"Listen, honey, I have some money put aside to help with your college expenses..." Stacy had told him about her scholarships and said his support wasn't needed. Another attempt to shut him out. But there were always extra expenses.

"Dad, I'm good. Jared's doing really well with his web company. Really well."

"Let me write you a check, anyway. Call it a Christmas gift. And I'll help with the wedding." He pressed a check for several thousand dollars into her hand. "I'll give you more when we get closer to your wedding. Keep me in the loop on your expenses." The fact that Cherie didn't need the college fund would definitely help his plan with Mavis. He made a mental note to write to her later.

The afternoon flew by. She promised to fly down for a week in March and bring Jared. He tapped his fingers on the table and debated, almost told Cherie about Olivia, but it was too new to share. Just after six, she drove away in the Mercedes belonging to her fiancé's parents.

He stood in the doorway filled with hope he hadn't known in years. Could he have a heart attack from pure joy? The greatest Christmas gift he could ever have, his child, was back in his life. She wanted him in hers.

He needed to move to burn off excitement and headed up to the main building with a spring in his step.

"Mr. Weston," Mrs. Paulson called over, "There's a package in the office for you."

*Huh? What'd be delivered on Christmas day?* He unlocked the office door, spotted the package on the chair, from Olivia, and opened it right there. When had she come by? Why didn't she stop down at the cottage? Now he regretted telling the dorm parents he didn't want to be disturbed. He unfolded the quilt to get a good look and warmed with admiration. Dark-green trim framed light-blue sections of alternating squares containing vines and watermelon slices embellished with embroidered black seeds. A work of art—she'd made it, he was sure. In the corner he found her initials and moved his thumb across their delicate stitching.

He brought the soft fabric to his face. Was he imagining, or could he detect her lavender scent? When was the last time he'd received such a thoughtful gift? If she were here, he'd gather her up and let her know how much he appreciated it. He tucked it under his arm and locked the office back up. After grabbing a carry out dinner in the dining hall, he'd head back to his empty cottage and give Olivia a call.

## 17

*A*lthough it was exactly the distraction Olivia needed, a marathon of Go Fish, Old Maid, and Candy Land wasn't how she'd originally envisioned spending her Christmas afternoon. Lindsay made the rounds, getting people to play.

She meant to turn away from the hurt inside by focusing on the games, but it leaked out anyway, making her short-tempered. She heard Blessie talking to Anna in the kitchen.

"Why's Olivia so grumpy?"

"It's a big change for her to be here this year. Perhaps she's a little blue."

She glanced over to meet Anna's worried look and slunk into the quiet den, her face stiff from forcing a smile all afternoon. Why was she on the verge of tears? She hardly knew Trevor, had no right to feel betrayed by him, but betrayal was rearing its ugly head. The nautical ornaments on the small tree brought up memories of the previous night when she'd felt cherished. This was a bad choice of a place to sit.

Mark poked his head in the room. "What's up, Livy Belle? Wanna talk?"

She shook her head. *No, not to Trevor's friend.* He lowered his large frame beside her, anyway. The two of them sat quietly, staring at the tree across the room. It was a comfort to have him beside her, probably like having a dad. Hers had left when she'd been born and she'd known Mark since grade school. He'd stood in for a father when she'd lived with them in high school and he'd grilled the boys she dated.

He leaned forward, placed his forearms on his knees, and spoke looking toward the tree, his discomfort palpable. "I know it must be difficult, what with the divorce."

"It's not that." She waved her hands. "Steele and I didn't have traditions."

"Anything you want to tell me about Steele?"

She stared at him a moment, searching his face, and swallowed against a lump in her throat. Mark couldn't know about Steele's temper and history of infidelity, could he? She trusted Tara.

"Tara told me about Steele, about the time he hurt you, and the women."

Couldn't she trust anyone? She tensed her jaw in anger. Tara was supposed to keep the secret, had promised not to spread it around like family gossip. Even her cousin had betrayed her. Despite her effort, her lids rimmed with tears.

Mark held her and stroked her hair like she'd seen him do with his kids a hundred times. For a moment she cried, making the shoulder of his shirt wet.

"Whatever happened up there, Livy Belle, you deserve better than that."

"Tara wasn't supposed to say anything." She palmed the tears off her face.

"Don't be pissed at her. She'd gotten into the spiked eggnog, and you know she can't hold a thimble-full of liquor. She meant well."

"Please promise you won't tell Anna. Steele's over a thousand miles away now, and she has enough to deal with. Anyway, that's not what's bothering me today."

He nodded. "I'll keep it to myself for now. But if that's not the issue, what is? This isn't about you and Trevor, is it? I noticed you two were in here for quite a while last night." He hissed a long breath through his teeth. "It seemed like you were getting along. He didn't do anything to bother you, did he? He's my friend, but I'll kill him if he hurt you." Mark lifted his forehead and held genuine concern on his face. He'd always been protective of her and hadn't approved of Steele, said Olivia was too good for him. When he'd gotten rough, Mark was the last person she'd tell. What would Mark do to Steele? Or Trevor, if he thought Trevor hurt her, even her feelings? He was an easygoing tech guy now, but at one time had been a wild and rough college football player with an attitude. Anna claimed to have tamed him.

"No, you don't have to kill Trevor, Mark. We had a misunderstanding. It's my own fault. I read too much into things."

"You didn't go out with him this afternoon. Anything you want to say about that?"

"No. I'll be okay." She tried to sound like she meant it but felt gutted.

Mark seemed to relax at closing the door on messy emotional talk. Feelings were Anna's department, and he got a lot of credit for making an effort this afternoon. But now Tara, her main confidant, was now on the list of people she couldn't trust.

～～～

The Christmas dinner table could have graced a magazine cover, but Olivia was just going through the motions. She kept the attention off herself by complimenting the centerpiece and Anna's lavish spread. The table groaned with crisp browned turkey, sage dressing, honey-crusted ham, potatoes au gratin, southern-style green beans, a basket of homemade rolls and corn muffins, and a big green salad with berries and nuts. But as she looked at it, her stomach burned and she felt a little ill. She couldn't even muster excitement for dessert, the cakes, and her favorite, pumpkin pie. Perhaps she could choke down a plate loaded with cheesy potatoes and buttery rolls—eating like a five-year-old.

"Interesting choice of food, El." Matthew teased her like a brother. Four years younger than her, they'd grown up together.

In no mood for teasing, she shot him a look. "Don't mess with me today."

Matthew gave her a sly grin. "You know what snowmen eat for Christmas dinner? Frosted flakes."

She rolled her eyes.

Lindsay giggled.

Matthew hiked his brows to his hairline and opened his lids so wide he looked like a total goofball. "What did one snowman ask the other snowman? Do you smell carrots?"

Natalie shook her head. "Don't laugh. You'll encourage him."

When the meal ended, she threw herself into cleanup like a woman on a mission. "Anna deserves a break after all the food prep."

She shooed her cousin to the breakfast bar with a cup of decaf while Mark and Matthew cleared the dining room table. When the guys stole off to watch TV, she and Natalie finished the kitchen.

"You want to tell us why you spent the afternoon playing cards with Lindsay? Not that I don't appreciate it, but I thought you had plans." Natalie paused from drying the pots and pans.

"Not really." Olivia schooled her face neutral.

"It might help to talk about it. Spill." Anna gave her the look that always made her cave.

She scoured the pan, finding it too difficult to meet their curious eyes. If only she could have a do-over for the day—better yet, a do-over for the decade. "I dropped off the watermelon quilt at the Center this afternoon. Trevor texted he needed to reschedule, and I thought it'd be a nice Christmas surprise. Mrs. Paulson locked it in the office for him." She rolled in her lips and bit them.

"Well, I'm sure he'll get it, Olivia." Anna flashed Natalie a puzzled look.

"That's not it. As I was leaving, I spotted him standing outside his house, hugging some skinny woman with long black hair. They seemed *very* friendly."

"Long black hair?" Anna tilted her head, got up, and came to the sink. She couldn't sit still that long.

"Yes. He put his arm around her and they walked into his cottage. Didn't Mark say he didn't have a girlfriend? I feel ridiculous giving him the quilt. But I couldn't take it back."

"As far as I know, that's true. I haven't heard of a girlfriend." Anna wrinkled her forehead. "Mark said he didn't think so. He does have a daughter. Mark's seen a photo of her. A cute blonde like Lindsay. I can't explain what you saw, Olivia, but if you're this fragile, sweetie, maybe it's too soon to think about dating."

She slowly nodded. The kitchen was spotless. What else could she do?

Natalie headed toward the family room. "Come on, Livy, watch *It's a Wonderful Life* with us."

She sat through about half the movie then headed to bed early. Tomorrow had to be better. Her phone needed to be put on the charger. *A voicemail from Trevor?* He'd called, and she'd missed it. No way could she take more drama tonight. Would he lie to her like Steele? There was a text from her mom: *Call me, honey.* Honey? That usually meant her mom wanted something. Nevertheless, she pressed Lydia's number. It was Christmas, after all.

"Cynthia called me, honey."

No telling what her sister had said. Traitor. Cynthia had always been a clone of their mother.

Lydia launched into a proposal. "One of Phillip's golfing buddies is a dean at Lone Star Academy. You have a shot at a job there, and they're interviewing next week to hire for the second semester. The dean owes Phillip a favor. One little problem—it's art history and humanities, not studio art—but you could adjust, right? I daresay it's cleaner and easier on the manicure. And they pay well for a private school. Plus, Phillip knows a gallery owner. If you send images of your art, they'll consider you for a show. I sent an email earlier with his contact. And it happens one of Phillip's partners has a nice-looking son, also an attorney, recently divorced." Lydia finally stopped.

There it was. Her stomach knotted, the main reason her mom wanted her to come out. Meet a nice attorney and get remarried to someone her mother approved of. Olivia should come out to live, Lydia said, right after the New Year. They would help her get things settled. They had it all figured out.

What should she say? For the most part, her mother's plan had merit. She'd never taught art history and didn't want to, but Lydia said it paid well. It was a job. Not entirely on her own merit, and she'd be beholden to Phillip. An art show? That wasn't a sure thing unless Phillip had pulled some strings, and he probably had. But her art was good. She'd been in shows with her paintings and her art quilts. Accepting Lydia's invitation meant moving to Texas, but that'd been her original idea. The offer probably came with a mandatory makeover. She'd meet the freshly divorced attorney if it kept her mom off her back. If she didn't want to date him, no doubt her mom would keep lining up eligible men until she found a suitable husband.

Despite preferring the tropical breezes of Florida, she could move. Mom was already checking flights. She'd sleep on it and get back to her in the morning. Tomorrow she'd also listen to Trevor's voicemail and respond. So many choices. None of them perfect, but least she'd be moving forward.

## 18

The morning cold pleasantly numbed Olivia as she sat on the patio watching the palm fronds flutter against a clear blue sky. After a night tossing and turning, weighing her options, she'd decided to take the interview in Dallas. Since her mom had been the one to reach out, she was spared from having to go crawling to her. What had Cynthia said that had prompted Lydia to call immediately?

In Dallas, she'd ask her stepfather for a loan to get out on her own and pay him back if she got hired. With that would come a steep price to pay. Lydia would expect to have veto power in her life. It took a lot of energy to ward off her mother's constant "helpful" meddling. A chronic disappointment to Lydia, there was no way she'd ever be a mini-me like Cynthia. They were velvet. She was chambray.

"Come to the beach with us, Liv." Matthew, already dressed in shorts, Birkenstocks, and a Falcons sweatshirt, poked his head out the sliding glass door. The brilliant sun would warm the day and promised every tourist's favorite December weather.

"No, you guys go ahead." She took another swig of bitter dark roast and winced, having skipped the sugar. It suited the mood that had followed her out of bed.

"Aw, come on, Livy. We hardly ever see you and look at this beautiful day." Matthew raised his palms. "You know you'll like it."

She gave him a suspicious sidelong glance. Anna must've said something for him to badger her.

"We're gonna go to the beach." Lindsay bounded around her father, holding up a blue plastic bucket and shovel, all smiles in her mermaid hoodie, shorts, and flip-flops. "Please, Olivia, come with us. We're making a sandcastle."

"It'd sure be nice to have an artist help us design the castle," Natalie called from the family room, where she packed a tote with towels, sunscreen, snacks, and waters.

"Okay, okay, I'll ride along." She pushed herself out of the chair. "Is Blessie coming?"

Mark glanced up from the recliner where he'd been working on his tablet. "She and Anna are baking more cranberry loaves. Blessie wants to give some to the dorm parents and she wants to get back for games in the community room. You go to the beach with Matthew and Natalie. Fresh air will improve your mood, Livy Belle."

Darn, she couldn't glare at Mark when he used his special name. She slipped into a gray sweatshirt and capris. Her gaze fell on the *No-Limits Holiday* book next to the bed and she snarled. *A lot of good it's done so far.* Couldn't she stick with a one-idea-a-day plan to improve her life? Letting out a deep sigh, she opened the book. "Do one thing different. Choose one new thought." She scowled at the page. *That's two things.* But probably pretty easy.

She glanced at her phone. Two voicemails from Trevor. And a text had come in asking her if they were still on. *On?* She should listen to her voicemails but her finger wouldn't press play. She was in no mood for lies, which pretty much eliminated anything Trevor might say, since her internal lie detector was broken. She stared at the phone.

A new text from Trevor pinged. *Pick you up for the beach at 1:00?*

*Pick me up?* The phone slipped from her hand like it burned her, then she grabbed it off the carpet. *Do one thing different?* Okay, she'd respond. *Can't go, busy.* There. That was different from ignoring his text. She resisted the urge to check his voice mail. Even though it made her stomach roil, she'd go cold turkey and drop this flirtation before it turned into something real and she got hurt.

The blame was partly on her. She'd come on too strong, giving him the quilt. And then he'd ditched her for that woman in the red dress. The heavy feeling of rejection and embarrassment weighed on her. It was possible this was more about Steele, but if Trevor managed to rouse these feelings, she ought to avoid men. She could, would, and already was dialing it back. Somehow, she'd muster up the courage to go to the Center and work tomorrow in spite of her misgivings. Olivia 2.0 would be strong.

She placed the phone on the bedside table, picked it up, put it back down. Why not go to the beach unplugged? That'd be another different thing for her. She grabbed her sunhat and pushed herself out the door.

What was she thinking? The beach was exactly where Olivia didn't want to be. December's wind blew chilly across the wide-open stretch of sand that could pass for snow. Crystal Sands offered a hundred yards of pristine sand stretching to blue-green water. People who wanted to be here would find it beautiful. She groaned. Why'd she let herself get talked into this? She was supposed to be here with Trevor—yesterday. Today, he'd hitchhiked along in her head. *Get out!* She pushed away the image of his face and gulped breaths of the salty air, focusing on her surroundings.

At the south end, over a mile down, sat a pavilion. Tourists packed that area despite the cool temperature. This end, still empty, required a special parking permit and had a wild patch of woods.

Olivia held Lindsay's little hand, trudging through the powdery sand relieved to reach the flat area about twenty yards back from the crashing surf.

They claimed their space with a blanket and chairs. Matthew and Lindsay took off on a shell hunt, and Natalie settled in with her book. Olivia stared at the horizon. The wide-open scene worked its magic and began melting away her tension.

Natalie set down her book. "Matthew said you practically lived at this beach back in high school. I can see why."

"True. Me and Madison and Lexie called ourselves the fearsome threesome. Lexie was going to the community college and she drove us everywhere. Right over there where the shoreline is flat and Matthew and Lindsay are hunting shells, Lexie'd whip down the beach on her skim board." She chuckled at the memory. "Those were the days—we had bonfires..."

"That's when your mom moved to Texas and you stayed here? What was Matthew like?"

"Yeah, high school... I liked living with them. Matthew liked fishing, playing football. Mark coached." Her gaze drifted in the direction of the pavilion where she'd worked at the concession around the time her mom had moved. Anna had never asked for her help, but her cousin had been swamped with teaching, raising two kids and helping Blessie. She'd fallen into picking up the slack, earning her keep, being agreeable. After all, her cousin didn't have to take her in.

Beyond the pavilion was the gazebo where she'd assisted when Blessie and Jennifer had come out for the special education department family picnics. All sorts of people attended: children in beach wheelchairs with giant plastic wheels, youngsters with leg braces, canes, even an older boy with a guide dog. She'd volunteered to serve food, had enjoyed helping Blessie, Jennifer, and others. That's probably why she'd decided to become a teacher.

White seabirds glided and called on the chilly breeze. Natalie joined Lindsay and stood in the water, scooping the sea floor, probably looking for sand dollars. Their ankles had to be freezing.

The sunshine warmed Olivia's face and the sound of the waves beating the shore lulled her into a relaxed state. Thinking became a chore. She breathed deeply, finally relaxed enough to observe the feelings tangled within her, sadness, embarrassment, anger, and regret. And more. Here in nature, she detected a subtle sense of peace spread out beneath all the other feelings.

Awareness of connection to the immensity of nature, the sky, the sand, and the water, opened within her. In this timeless place she felt small, yet part of something greater. The same strong person she'd been growing up was there beneath the drama of her recent past. She refused to be defeated by her experiences and wouldn't allow feelings of rejection to define her.

Disappointment and grief had blanketed her like a fog bank. But fog evaporated in the light of sun. Fog could be moved through to the other side, where it was clear again. On the other side of her fog bank, she'd create a new life.

"Olivia, are you ever gonna get up? We're making the sandcastle. Come and help." Lindsay grabbed her hand. She jerked back to reality and allowed her little cousin to pull her to her feet.

Matthew moved her chair over to the sandcastle construction zone and winked. "In case you need to sit." He headed to the surf to grab a bucket of water. "Hey, look!" He pointed offshore. "Dolphins. Check it out." They gathered next to Matthew and watched the dolphins surface and submerge, dorsal fins rolling through the aquamarine waves over and over. There were four, maybe five of them. After a couple of minutes, the marine mammals swam too far out to see.

She walked back to the sandcastle area, her step lighter. Natalie handed her a metal garden trowel. "Ready to build something?"

Olivia took the tool and began to dig. Yes, definitely ready to start building something. But what, and where?

## 19

*T*his would be a great day. Trevor was still high from seeing Cherie, and now he'd see Olivia. He savored his hot coffee in the cool morning on the concrete pad behind the cottage. As he stretched his long legs out, he leaned back, satisfied. The rose bushes, loaded with buds, hadn't gotten hit by the cold. He'd likely cut dozens more blooms before pruning them next month.

The day after Christmas, the effects of the cold front were fading into the type of weather that prompted people to move to Florida. Vapor steamed from the damp ground between the palmettos and pines creating a mystical effect in the forest behind his cottage. Molly sniffed around for lizards. Today would be a good day for a drive to the key, possibly have a late lunch at that seafood place on the water. He should call for a reservation. The clock said nine. Not too early to contact Olivia about this afternoon. He broke into a satisfied grin when he recalled how much he enjoyed being with her. It'd be sweet to sit together at the beach, listen to the surf, and enjoy warm sunshine in the cool breeze. But he hadn't heard a thing from her, so he sent her a text. While he waited to hear back, he grabbed himself another cup of coffee and then checked the phone again. No text. He called and left a voicemail. In the meantime, he had work to do.

About 10:30, he sent another text, and right away his phone pinged. A text from Olivia. *Can't go, busy.* He stared at the screen. That seemed curt. Also, no response to the two voicemails and earlier text he'd left Christmas and this morning. Skilled at reading his students, but a woman he wanted to date—not so much. But that text seemed cold. Why? He'd left a message last night and had thanked her for the quilt, said he wanted to talk. She hadn't returned his call. He shook his head, confused, stepped into the greenhouse, and began working.

After eleven, he texted back, *Reschedule? I love the quilt, it's beautiful.*

He dove into his work, organized, and cleaned, stopping to check his phone several times. Nope. Nothing. *Is she angry?* For the life of him, he couldn't figure out why she'd be upset unless it was because he'd rescheduled their beach date. He should've made the time to ring her up Christmas morning. But he'd gotten busy helping with the breakfast.

She'd left that beautiful quilt, and now silence. That didn't add up.

Maybe he'd come on too strong Christmas Eve. She'd seemed to like it, but what did he know? Somehow, he'd blown it. Two unanswered calls and texts and not much else. He could take a hint. He ground his teeth back and forth and decided to shove the situation out of his head. And all the confusing feelings that went with it could go too.

Already one-thirty, time had flown by as Trevor had thrown himself into mucking out the stable and feeding the horses and was now back at the greenhouse. He pushed thoughts of Olivia from his mind. The meeting tomorrow required a clear head. After the greenhouse, he'd work on paperwork. Mavis had pulled some strings, applied pressure, and they'd scheduled a board meeting for Monday afternoon. The two of them were presenting their alternative plan, and he needed to be at the top of his game. But his mind kept drifting back to Olivia. Should he drive over and see her in person? This was exactly why he hadn't wanted to get involved with a woman. It's drama he didn't need.

A cheerful voice broke through his dark mood. "Wow. Look at all the pots. You put out the little ones for new seeds." Blessie was coming through the doorway, her usual smiling self, poking around the new eight packs. "Are we getting ready to plant the seeds?" She wandered down to the far end, sticking her fingers in the pots as she moved along.

Mark's linebacker profile filled the entrance to the greenhouse, having just caught up with Blessie. "Hey, Trevor, what's up?" His friend set a bag on the floor and stood staring, hard jaw thrust forward.

He began to answer then paused, glimpsing his friend's tight expression, considering his odd tone. *Is Mark angry about something?* He moved the bag of potting soil under the table. "Almost got it organized for planting." He waved at the starter pots stretched for forty feet on the tables.

"Looks like you've been busy." Mark sounded like he was holding back. A moment of uncomfortable silence stretched between them.

"How's Olivia today?" *Crap.* It slipped out. What's wrong with him? Mark didn't deserve to be put in the middle. But they might as well broach the issue.

"She's fine, I guess... at the beach with Matthew and Natalie. They left a while ago." Mark cast him a sidelong glance.

"Where?" His tone was sharp. He met Mark's gaze, then stared at the ground, a strange knot in his stomach. She was at the beach... not with him. Yep. This was why he had no business even thinking about Olivia. Women were fine for friends but try to date one and look what happened.

"Olivia was really down yesterday." Mark leveled a dark look his way. "You two seemed to hit it off the other night." He paused. "Got any ideas what happened?"

Mark clenched his hand. His friend was pissed.

He took off his gloves, shoved them in his back pocket, and studied the man. Never one to wear his heart on his sleeve, he didn't know how much he wanted to say to his friend, who was, after all, Olivia's family.

"Yep, I thought we were hitting it off. Olivia's a nice woman. I enjoyed spending time with her. You've got a great family." There. That settled it.

"Anna said you and Olivia had plans." Mark turned to the side, moved a planter, and released a loud breath. "Everything all right?"

"I asked Olivia out. You okay with that?"

The big guy shrugged. "Sure. She's a grown woman." His gaze flashed a warning. "She's been through a lot, more than you'd know." Mark's head drifted up and down and his jaw ticked.

"Point taken." Exactly what point was unclear since he'd done nothing out of line. Now his head was starting to throb. *Damn confusing mess.* Mark probably wanted him to back off. How could he *back off* when he couldn't even *find his way on?* She was ignoring him. Mark needed to chill. He'd deescalated raging residents and could deal with his friend. "Things are okay here. Good even." He shut off the hose, changed the subject. "Yesterday, Cherie came by for the afternoon." Happiness spread through him simply saying it aloud.

"Your Cherie? Your daughter?" Mark's tone brightened as he took a few steps inside the greenhouse.

"Yep, surprised me." He lifted one shoulder. "I tried to reschedule with Olivia, left a message." He groaned. Here he was, having to explain himself. "It was good to see my daughter."

"Humph." Mark shoved his hands in his pockets, looking

relieved to find neutral ground. "Yeah, great to see your kid. Were you expecting her?"

"Nope. But I'll be seeing more of her. She asked me to be there when she gets married in June. And she might move down for grad school. Cherie applied to the veterinary program in Florida."

Mark clapped him on the back, friendlier now. "Hey, man, that's great." He jerked his head toward Blessie, who was down at the far end of the greenhouse. "I didn't mean to bring her out here to disturb you." He shouted. "Hey, Blessie, let's go."

Trevor watched them walk toward the rear doors of the main building, Mark carrying a big bag of baked goods alongside Blessie, shorter, with her unmistakable energetic step. He noted a pang of jealousy. Wouldn't it be good to have a family like that, where people looked out for each other? Seemed like they had so much love they could spread it around. At least Cherie was in his life again. Her visit in March couldn't come fast enough, and he'd meet Jared then too. He headed to his cottage to talk to Mavis and strategize. If he prepped enough, thinking about tomorrow's meeting might stop churning up his gut.

～～～～

Mark was especially quiet tonight. Anna'd noticed his brows drawn together over dinner and wished he'd simply tell her what was wrong. After dinner, they said goodbye to Matthew and his family, then cleaned the kitchen in companionable silence. He dried pans and handed them to her, a team. More than married, they were friends.

Her husband had celebrated his fifty-eighth birthday last month. She wished Olivia would stay, so they'd be able to slip away on the road trip he'd been dreaming about.

"Did Tara mention anything to you about Steele or the night Olivia got hurt?" His nostrils flared, getting worked up.

"What are you talking about?"

"Never mind. I'm just glad that jerk's not in her life anymore. I think if he showed his face, I'd have to rip his head off." They worked in silence for a minute but by the way he attacked the pots with that towel, he was still angry. "Trevor had a visit from his daughter. Looks like he'll walk her down the aisle when she gets married in June."

"That's nice for Trevor." Anna's tone was cool. "You know, Olivia saw him hugging someone with long black hair when she dropped off a gift for him. Right outside his cottage at the same time they were supposed to go out together. It really upset her."

"Humph. And Olivia brought him a gift? He didn't say anything about that. Cherie's a blond, far as I know. But he said she stopped by." Mark set down his towel and drew Anna close, squeezing her tight. "Sweetheart, I'm so glad we're married. It's much less confusing."

"Less confusing than what?" She laughed, then dropped her jaw. "Do you remember that horrible phase when Stephanie dyed her hair black? Trevor didn't show you a recent photo of Cherie, did he? Was that his daughter with black hair?"

"Don't meddle, sweetheart. Olivia's mood seemed better tonight."

She regarded her husband and groaned. "I need more facts. My image of Trevor... I'm disappointed. I'll feel better knowing he's not a jerk." He was, after all, an important part of Blessie's life.

## 20

*O*livia's finger hovered over the smooth screen of her phone as she debated calling out sick. Between the enormous book of accommodations she'd never master in a week, and the chance of running into Trevor, it was tempting. But she'd given Jeanette her word. Dread filled her as she drove to the Center. When she arrived midday, she briskly picked up the key and scurried down the hall into the art room without seeing him.

In the immaculate space, supplies were easy to find and she set up for painting. She meant to avoid looking out the window toward Trevor's cottage, but the horses out back caught her eye. Volunteers had youngsters brushing the tan one and the mini horse that Blessie loved. Trevor stood with them, too dressed up to be doing outdoor work. He must be going somewhere. Watching him filled her with longing.

A knock on the door brought her back to the room, and she welcomed her four students.

"Paints!" Terrance ran to his seat and grabbed the brush.

For the next hour, the students mixed colors and painted with tempera paints.

"Josie, these pictures are so colorful. May I frame one to hang in the hall?" Together they picked one out for display, and the girl's grin went straight to her heart.

The second class needed acrylic plates and brayers. The print-making technique, similar to finger painting, should be fun for the students who didn't have good fine motor control. Caught up in possibilities for her students, she detected a pang of regret. *It's only a temp job—one, two weeks tops.*

Monday morning Trevor had nearly worn out the floor of his cottage pacing. The light holiday schedule this week meant too much time on his hands. When he'd told Jeanette about Olivia, he hadn't foreseen wanting to start something up with her and things getting complicated. This was why he had a policy about dating coworkers. Who needed the mess that arose when things turned bad? Now she'd be here all week. He'd get through it. If he ran into her, he'd keep it professional and he was typically outdoors anyway.

He was talking to volunteers at the stable when he spotted the light come on in the art room across the campus. Olivia was here. The urge to go see her gripped him. He placed his focus on the group before him but his gaze kept wandering across the grounds to the art room.

The situation at the Center was too important for him to be distracted; it'd make or break the programs he'd built. He went inside and fixed lunch but a gnawing sensation worked over his gut. Molly whined, picking up on his mood. He pulled a slice of chicken out of his sandwich for her then tossed the remainder in the trash, his stomach too tight to eat.

When he strode up to the main building for the board meeting, he couldn't avoid walking by the art room. He peered through the window on the door. Olivia, oblivious to him, was working with a group of smiling kids doing something with brayers, paint, and tissue paper, kind of like finger painting. They were having a ball. Even Brandon, who had the brace on his arm, could do it. She seemed so patient. The corner of his mouth turned up. Awkward or not, it was the right call to have her here. Too bad Jeanette wasn't around to see this.

"Ready for the meeting?" Mavis's voice came from behind.

He tensed. She'd caught him spying like a love-struck high school boy.

"Yes. Just checking on our new art teacher sub."

"I see."

They moved down the hall and strategized in the conference room. The closing for the sale of the northeast acreage was scheduled for Friday morning. The plan was to garner the votes necessary to cancel or revise the sale.

He hammered his heel on the floor, nerves getting the best of him. "You spent all day yesterday winning Willis and Daniels?" Pastor Don was already on their side.

"Let's say I can be persuasive. And I have this file I printed with the report from Granite Solutions." She opened the envelope on the table and removed a stack of papers.

He cast an appreciative eye at the handsome woman with a resolute expression sitting across from him. *Thank God she's an ally.*

Mavis took a sip of coffee and leveled a serious look his way. "Trevor." Her voice held uncharacteristic firmness. "Listen. We have a plan. A good plan. But that doesn't mean it'll work. I've called in favors, applied leverage, but it's not a sure thing." She sighed. "Sometimes things don't go the way we want."

A coil of anxiety contracted his chest. *What's she holding back?*

"You're well liked here and do a great job with the garden, the horses, and the residents."

"Yes?" The coil around his chest tightened. *Where's the "but?"* This sounded like something they'd say before handing you a pink slip.

"You deserve this plan to go through." A long moment of silence stretched between them.

"And? It sounds like there's more." He drummed his fingers lightly on the side of his mug.

"I may be overstepping my bounds, but humor an old woman, please."

He nodded and tried to keep his voice neutral. "All ears."

"You're working here weekends, evenings, holidays. I admire what a great job you've done for more than a decade. Perhaps too good a job. There are other things in life. You're not an old man. I know you were married once. I met your daughter several years ago, and you tell me she came by on Christmas. That's great. But kids grow up. They have their own lives, and rightly so. I notice things, Trevor. I don't miss much."

He studied the dark liquid in his mug. *Where's she going with this?* He braced himself.

"I don't see you dating or with family. You're married to the job here, married to the garden, the people, the Center. It good for the Center. It's nice to know you're around when we need you. But. I wonder, how good is it for you?"

Whoa, not what he expected. "Well, Mavis—"

She held up her hand, stopping him. "I loved Rodney, God rest his soul. It was long and enduring. He was my friend, my husband, my partner. When things on the outside fall apart, as they're known to do, you need something to fall back on. There's faith. Of course, there's faith." Mavis paused.

He was silent.

"But faith doesn't keep you warm at night. We need faith and, especially at your age, a partner's good too. You're still young. Me and my Rodney spent many a quiet evening on the terrace drinking sherry at sunset, reviewing our day. It's the little moments together that add up to a lifetime of companionship. I'd like that for you. Trevor, you're a good man and could use a life mate. The Center here, well, it may go on for years. It may not—we just don't know.

You have all your eggs in this basket. I want you to have what Rodney and I had. I want that for you too, dear. I caught the way you were watching that woman temping in the art room before the meeting today. Would that be a good place to start?" Mavis was silent, raised her brow, and peered at him expectantly.

*Where does she get off telling me?* He pressed his lips into a hard line but had the oddest feeling of familiarity. Grandma Paula's wisdom and concern seemed to have flowed straight through Mavis. He wanted to resist, to argue for his choices, but she was right. He gave a hundred ten percent to this place and now faced cutbacks that could put him right out of a job.

After seeing Cherie on Christmas Day, and Olivia Christmas Eve, he'd come alive, like finding green inside a tree that appeared to be dead wood. He was ready for a change. Getting booted out of a job he loved wasn't it. For things with Olivia to go awry so soon was a punch in the gut, but when you open your heart to caring, that's the risk you take.

If the meeting today didn't go as planned, if he wound up out of a job and moved away from the cottage, he'd deal with it. He'd touched lives, had done good. But what would he have left? Cherie was in his life now but soon she'd be a married woman. Jared was her priority. That's the plight of fathers. Mavis had a point. Whatever happened in the meeting, things would be different after it. He wanted more. He wanted it all.

The clatter of footsteps and voices in the hall announced the other board members before they poured into the conference room. Mavis glanced his way, sat strong as an oak, and nodded. They held a few aces, and this afternoon they'd play them.

Slimy Smith, first through the doorway, scoffed in Trevor's direction. "What's he doing here?"

~~~~~~

Olivia stood at the doorway and welcomed her final group of the day, three boys. Lionel, a young man about seventeen who'd been away for the past month, entered the room last. The dorm parent introduced him to Olivia and left. He sat quietly while she demonstrated the oil pastel drawing technique. He frowned, brooded and didn't seem the least bit interested in making anything.

"I don't wanna draw. Where's Mrs. Carroll? When's she coming back?" He pushed away from the table.

"Like Miss Alma said, she's not here anymore. But I'm sure we can find something fun for you to do."

He scowled and ripped up his paper. Then he launched out of his seat and stormed around the room, opening and shutting cabinets with violent force. "I want Mrs. Carroll. Where is she?"

Her heart picked up. It'd been a long time since she'd had to deal with this kind of outburst. She spoke to him with a gentle tone, but he became more agitated and turned over a table holding books.

She glanced at the panic button on the wall. Should she push it or should she call Trevor? No, Mr. Perez, the music teacher, was across the hall. He picked up on the first ring and sent an assistant right over to help.

Familiar with Lionel, the assistant convinced him to give her a chance. By the time class was over, he was smiling, proudly holding up an oil pastel drawing, looking to her for approval. That turned out to be her favorite class of the day. She'd met the challenge with a positive outcome.

It was incredible how the time flew by when you were into art. She'd been able to sit part of the afternoon, and her foot didn't feel bad at all. This confirmed she'd be okay if she got that position in Dallas. With a light step, she locked up and left, congratulating herself on a good first day. And she'd managed to avoid meeting face to face with Trevor. Hopefully, her luck would last.

~~~~

Seth Smith had initially thrown up roadblocks, trying to comman-
deer the board meeting and railroad through the upcoming sale.
Trevor pulled up the security video, showing the unscrupulous
board member rifling through the files on the night of the twenty-
third. Mavis laid out the information Grant had dug up, showing
connections to the developer. She put forth a motion to ask for his
resignation. Smith reddened, muttered, and slammed the door as
he left.

A head for finance had given Trevor the edge to see possibilities. They got what they needed. Acreage would still be sold, but
only enough to build a back road for the development. The east
greenhouse and shed would need to come down and new ones
built on the other side of the garden. Since Cherie didn't need his
help, he'd been able to free up more funds than he'd originally
planned and provided a generous endowment. He'd purchased and
donated back a chunk of land the developer wanted, retaining
ownership of an acre. Mavis matched his donation.

Next, Mavis brought up the empty arts and crafts teacher position. Since the finances looked better, she wanted a certified
educator in the position. Funds for a part-time teacher were
approved. Then she cast Trevor a sly glance. "Since Mr. Weston has
an interest in the place and we're very grateful to him for granting
such a generous endowment, I move we fill the vacant board seat
with Trevor Weston. If he's willing to step up."

The vote was unanimous, the meeting adjourned, and the other
board members left. When the last of them cleared the doorway,
Mavis raised a palm for a high five. "Now you really are married to
the place," she teased, gathering her files. "But remember, there's
more to life than work."

Cherie's face flashed in Trevor's mind. *She's right.* The side of his
mouth edged up. His daughter would occupy part of his life now.
But she's getting married and had her own life. What about Olivia?
It annoyed him like hell that she ignored him. Yet, he still wanted
her. Mavis had nailed it. It'd been difficult for him to pull away

from watching her through the door. Was there any chance with her? Had he come on too strong and scared her off? Was she feeling broken from her divorce? Was he...too old for her? She was probably several years younger than him.

Well, there were more fish in the sea if he was looking. Now that his job was secure maybe he oughta look. It might be better for his friendship with Mark if ... he searched elsewhere. The problem was, he wanted Olivia. She lit fire in him in a place he'd thought was ashes. Protectiveness, passion, respect, she brought out all those feelings, surprising, since he'd only been with her a few times. But when you got to his age, the heart knows what it wants. He'd confront her, whatever it took.

He strode down the hall. The art room was already dark and locked. Damn, he'd missed her. With swift strides he headed toward the rear door, he'd hop in his Jeep and go after her.

Crash. "Ouch!" Crying.

"Mr. Weston. Mr. Weston, can you come help me get Len up? He may be injured." Mrs. Paulson waved for him to help.

He whipped his head in her direction and hustled down to check on Len. Finding Olivia would have to wait.

## 21

"*I*sn't it too cold to go out on the water?" Olivia pulled on her hoodie and slid into the car with Jennifer and Lexie. They were meeting Jennifer's friends Sami and Willow at the marina.

"That's why I said to bundle up. The wind will be chilly," Lexie explained as she steered in the direction of Salt Bay.

"I thought you said Madison was coming." Disappointment laced Olivia's tone. She'd hoped to spend more time with the cousin she'd been closest to growing up. They were even in some high school classes together.

Lexie puffed a breath. "It's as though she's working two jobs. She'd been running herself ragged with sewing commissions in the evenings. It's no wonder she's been irritable. She doesn't get any sleep." She cut Olivia a sly glance. "Somehow we'll manage to have fun without her."

They parked under tall pines and strolled down to the pier at Hidden Cove Marina. Introductions were made, and Willow showed them where to sit. An ecotour guide and marine science intern, her Christmas gift to Jennifer had been certificates for free charters.

"Hold on to your hats." Willow powered up the boat.

Olivia pulled her knit cap down around her ears as they motored toward the sun hanging low in the sky. "I've never seen the sunset from a boat before."

"You're in for a treat." Lexie handed over a fuzzy throw to drape across her knees. The wind went right through her leggings.

The boat planed over quicksilver green water with the cool salt-water breeze pinking their cheeks. Willow took the short route across the bay to the Colorfish Keys, a pair of dolphins trailing in their wake. She cut the engine at the mouth of a channel. "This is where I tell you about the birds, and we drift and use the quieter trolling motor."

"This is where *I* open the wine." Lexie grinned unabashedly. "Or we have decaf with Irish cream liqueur or hot chocolate. Take your pick."

"And I brought snacks." Sami held up bags of cheese, crackers, and nuts.

Drinks were poured and food passed around.

Olivia sipped her decaf with liqueur; the sweet warmth burned a little going down. "Whoa. I see something over there." She pointed.

Willow turned off the trolling motor and shifted into her ecotour guide role. "Yes. It's a manatee. Pretty soon they'll be swimming into the creeks and rivers. They prefer the warmer water this time of year. Some people think they're unintelligent, but it's not true. They may have the lowest brain-to-body ratio of any marine creature, but they've been shown to be as capable as dolphins in many experiments."

"Cool." Sami peered off the bow for a closer look.

Olivia leaned over the edge. "I've seen those off Mark and Anna's dock before." Memories of hanging out on the dock and appreciating the wildlife at different times of the year played across her mental screen. She'd forgotten how close to nature she felt down here. She glanced at Jennifer. Too bad her cousin couldn't see the manatee. "Are you having fun, Jen?"

"Sure. I love the smell of the saltwater, and going fast, and feeling the wind on my face. It's exhilarating."

Willow gestured to a thicket off the bow. "Look—over there, those trees. That's a place where the herons and egrets roost at night. They're already gathering. They prefer trees to the ground, where they're vulnerable to land predators."

Olivia leaned back, let the tension drain out of her neck, and enjoyed the tour. Hanging out with family and friends, watching the sky go from blue to orange to violet and the sun drop into the smooth water was pure bliss. When was the last time she'd had so much fun and been this relaxed?

Sami turned to Lexie. "When's Zach coming back? Brice has another project for him. We're remodeling the smaller barn. Making a studio."

"Speaking of Brice, have you two set a wedding date yet?" Lexie cocked her head.

"No. And I was asking *you* about Zach." Sami's tone had an edge.

"He's staying in Albuquerque an extra week. I guess he's having a great time." Lexie's flashed a mischievous smile in the fading light. "What I want to know is, how things are going with Olivia and Trevor?"

"Trevor? Trevor Weston?" Sami's gaze snapped over, wide-eyed. "Are you seeing him?"

Sami's tone brought Olivia upright and anxiety edged out her peace. "No, I'm not seeing him. I think he has a girlfriend." How had they gotten on this subject? She groaned.

"I doubt that." Sami snorted. "He... had a bad divorce, according to Brice. I didn't think he dated. Not that he talks about it much."

"Well, I saw him with someone. We're not a thing." And there it was. Trevor, circling around in her mind, taking up space in a place that five minutes ago had been blissfully empty.

## 22

The next morning Olivia backed away from the laptop and sat taller. On paper she looked good. The art files were polished to send and her resume glowed on the screen broadcasting accomplishments, reminding Olivia 2.0 this was a new chapter. Tired of sitting at a fork in the road, a quick press of the send key started her on the path undesired, but secure. A possible full-time job. She was warming up to the idea of moving to Dallas.

Now she had to tell Anna. It wasn't that she didn't want to stay. But getting caught up helping Blessie when her own life was a mess didn't make sense. What if Anna and Mark liked traveling? If she stayed to be a guardian for Blessie, then later found a job where she needed to commute, she'd wind up letting them all down. "The resume's looking good. I'm ready to put myself out there."

"You got it done?" Anna scanned the document on the screen. "Wow look at you! Awards for teaching and for art quilts. Second place at the Quilt Guild show two years ago? How did I not know that?"

Pride lifted her chest, and she grinned. She'd gotten accustomed to downplaying her wins. Steele was too competitive to appreciate her talent.

Anna brought over a tray of cranberry bread, cookies, and mugs of steaming apple cinnamon tea. "I'm glad to see you taking action. Didn't Jennifer say you could teach at the studio?"

"Yes, mentioned it." She tensed, uncomfortable, since she'd already texted her mom that morning regarding airline schedules. Pushing away the sweets, she resolved to reduce her sugar intake and enjoy the cinnamon scent of the tea. "On Christmas Eve Jen told me I had a big influence on her becoming a potter. I never knew." Her mind drifted to Trevor who'd sat on the other side of her Christmas Eve. His kisses were remarkable. She hadn't had kisses affect her like that since, well, before Steele. She pushed the thought away and focused on the view of tall white egrets wading in the creek.

"She always did look up to you. We never know when a simple comment or action creates a ripple effect in someone else's life." Anna picked cranberries out of a slice of bread. "I know you didn't ask, but I think the best course of action is for you to stay here, find a job, help with Blessie and house sit this summer. Forget about dating for a while."

She felt her forehead gather and jaw tense at Anna's controlling words.

"On the other hand, there's something Mark told me Sunday night about Trevor's daughter visiting. Did you know she visited?"

"No."

"Wasn't that quilt with the watermelons you brought him, the one you took the prize with?"

"Yes..." She drew out the syllable, and cringed, nodding slowly.

"Instead of selling that quilt, you gave it to Trevor. You must think very highly of him." Anna gave her a meaningful look.

She released a long breath. Heat filled her cheeks. Why had she been so impulsive? "I guess I was caught up in the moment."

"I told you not to go. I hated seeing you so disappointed."

Yep, there's the first *I told you so*, but she had to admit, Anna'd called it correctly. She'd been crushed Saturday afternoon.

"Mark said you and Trevor were awfully cozy in the den Christmas Eve."

She slathered butter on cranberry bread, giving in to a sudden urge to cram it in her mouth. *Just get to the point.* She already knew she'd made a mistake.

"Mark said Trevor had a visitor on Christmas—his daughter surprised him. What if that was his daughter with him on Saturday afternoon?"

She stopped chewing and dropped the bread. "Mark said she's a little blond like Lindsay."

"The photos Mark's seen were very old. Those are what he refers to when he says she looks like Lindsay. Remember when Stephanie colored her hair black?"

"I don't know what excuse I'd use to find out. It's too late. I didn't even speak to him yesterday." She scrolled through her text messages, a reality check. Yes, she'd been abrupt and chilly, hadn't responded to most of his texts, and his voicemails were still waiting. By now, he was rightly thinking she was avoiding him.

"Why do you need an excuse? Just ask. He's demonstrated a lot of understanding with Blessie." Anna sighed deeply. "Sometimes truth is the best course of action. I'm not saying I want you to rush into anything, but if he means something to you, clear things up. At least be friends—for Blessie's sake?" A moment ticked by. "Against my better judgment, if you want something with Trevor, I won't be the one to stand in your way. Does he have any idea how upset you were?" Anna squeezed her arm and left her alone to stew.

The coward's path, avoiding Trevor, would be easier. She wanted things clear with him but what if that hadn't been his daughter? There was a fine line between trusting and gullible. Her mouth went dry thinking about the confrontation. But if she took more risks, and spoke up for herself, she might get what she wanted more often. She was strong enough. Hadn't she packed her car and driven down the road without having a clue what was on the horizon? That took courage. Trevor was Blessie's teacher and

Mark's friend. Sometime in the next few days, she'd do the right thing and clear the air—for Blessie's sake.

≈≈≈

In the mild morning, Trevor and Brice crouched around the Sunshine Blue blueberry bushes the farmer had brought over. The man had written a book on berries and had a popular blog. Trevor considered himself lucky to count the guy as a friend. The semi dwarf shrubs looked healthy.

"They can produce with as little as a hundred fifty hours of chill." Brice stood back and nodded at the eight bushes he was donating. "I'm putting in a row to see how they do."

"Thanks. I'm looking to expand. Got those Jewel bushes in last week."

They wandered back to his friend's truck. Brice cut him a sidelong glance. "Sami says you're seein' someone?"

His pulse jumped. "What?" Why'd Brice care, and what in the hell was he talking about?

"Yep, someone Sami was with last night said she saw you looking mighty friendly with a woman on Christmas day. Drama, gossip. I don't usually pay it any mind."

"No. I'm not seeing someone." *Not for lack of trying.* He studied Brice a moment. The man was close to his own age and had recently moved to the area because of a woman. "But my daughter stopped by on Christmas. Who was saying?" He lowered his brow, tense, frustrated. His personal life was nobody's business.

"Some cousin of Sami's friend, Jennifer. I think. Never mind. Didn't mean to be nosy." They talked about the work Brice was doing at his new farm, and after a while, his friend got in his truck and drove off.

*Cousin of Jennifer? Not Blessie. She was gone on Christmas. Olivia? Olivia saw me with Cherie when she brought the quilt?* Was that why she's ignoring him? Tonight he'd get her alone and talk to her.

~~~~~

Before she left for work, Olivia found Anna on the back porch read-ing. "I need to tell you something." She gathered her courage. "I have a job interview next Tuesday in Dallas."

"You sent your resume to someone in Dallas? I thought you didn't want to live with your mom and Phillip."

"There's a full time position available. Phillip will give me a loan." If the position in Dallas fell through, staying with Anna and Mark until the end of January might work. But then she'd go. Dallas had a lot going for it. She'd focus on the positive. Her brother, Connor, enjoyed living there, although he was much older and very busy at the hospital. And of course—she cringed—there'd be Cynthia.

She surveyed the tropical landscaping of Anna's yard, inhaling the sweet scent of flowers. Valencia Cove was tempting, but she could get used to living somewhere else. With her head down and the window blinds shut, she'd get through the week and leave. It could work.

~~~~~

It wasn't unusual for Trevor to be called to do light maintenance when they were shorthanded. He could fix just about anything and wasn't surprised when they asked him to check on a clogged drain in the art room. It already felt like Olivia's space, and his heart sped up being in there. She'd reported the stopped up drain yesterday before leaving, but the office hadn't gotten the message to him until an hour ago.

Although it was his lunch time, he'd slip in, check it out, and be gone before she got there. Later he'd stop by and ask her to dinner so they could talk and pick up where they'd left off Christmas Eve.

The problem was the clay trap beneath the sink. The sucker hadn't been cleaned out in a while. He almost had it back in position when keys jangled in the art room door. Hell, it was only 12:30. Her class didn't begin until one. As soon as she stepped into the room, his breathing changed. Dammit. This wasn't how he planned to reconnect with her. He tamped down his excitement.

She swung open the door.

He slid out from underneath the sink, stood, and ran the water. "You're all set."

She hurried to the desk, put down the tote and notebook, and began moving papers, keeping her head down.

Undeterred, he moved to the edge of her desk. "Olivia," he whispered, mouth dry, hands in his pockets. Close enough to enjoy the clean scent of her shampoo, he fought back the urge to bring his face to her neck and bury it in her soft hair.

She kept her attention fixed on her paperwork. "Thank you, I appreciate your doing that. I didn't expect the office to call you."

"Edgar took a long weekend for the holiday. I help out when he's gone." He paused. She finally raised her head and their eyes locked, but neither spoke. He searched her face, leaned forward, kissing distance, began to speak, but was instantly interrupted.

"Ms. Brighton, is it okay if we come in early?" Mrs. Paulson followed Richie, in his wheelchair, already halfway into the room.

He swallowed his frustration and slipped into the helpful-colleague mode. "Happy to do it. Let me know if there's anything else you need." He started toward the door, stopping to fist bump Richie on his way out.

There were so many things he should've said to Olivia. He needed to connect with her and get it right. But since one of the volunteers had called in sick, he was spending the afternoon in the thera-peutic riding program. His assistant, Wren, had the first riders in the tack room going over the bridles and saddles while he got ready.

About the time the horses were saddled, Tammi came out with a stack of chocolate chip cookies and cold drinks and stayed longer than necessary. The muscles in his face tightened as he struggled to be polite. The kids just wanted to climb on the horses and she was holding things up. She sashayed over to him and leaned forward. It appeared she'd missed a couple of the buttons at the top of her shirt. He refused to let his gaze linger there. Next, the well-endowed dining room manager surprised him by resting her hands on his arm as she spoke, as though touching him was normal. Tensing under her hold, he took a step back and kept things professional. What was that about? She knew he wasn't interested. He helped the kids up and started the lesson. Finally Tammi left.

Wren rolled her eyes, flashed him a wry half smile and led Winnie, who carried a visually impaired youngster on her back. His rider, a tiny little redhead with sensory integration issues, had climbed on Brink, smiling wide, patting his neck. Two more children were scheduled after them. When riding time ended, the youngsters watered the horses and helped brush them down. Although it flowed smoothly, by the time they filled out paperwork, took care of the horses, and had the gear put away, Olivia was gone.

Back in his cottage he sat on his couch, staring out the window at the main building. Last night he'd spent several hours with Leonard at the emergency room, sidelining his plan to see Olivia. They'd put a cast on the young man's broken arm. Then he'd stopped and bought the kid an ice cream on the way back to the Center.

Across the campus, the art room sat dark and empty and the need to take action gnawed at him. He grabbed his keys, drove to Mark's house and knocked on the door—no more relying on texts and calls she could ignore. Christmas lights lit the place up, but the windows were dark and the Ram was gone. They'd gone out. Just to be sure, he tried the doorbell. Nothing. Either he'd missed Olivia, or she was hiding out, avoiding him. He sat in the driveway, trying to come up with a Plan B. Deflated, he turned the Jeep around and drove back to the center. He needed a better idea, something that worked. Soon.

ow was it Wednesday already? Olivia stopped in Jake & Jen's Café & Clay to meet Tara for lunch before going into work. "Hi, Dominic. It's nice to see you're still working here."

"How're you doing, Olivia?" The café manager, whose deep voice still had a touch of a Jamaican accent, greeted her from the stool behind the counter where he was tapping numbers into a laptop.

Her phone buzzed. A text from Tara. *Appointment's running late. I need to cancel. So sorry. Meet up later this week?*

She'd have to eat alone. Her *No-Limits Holiday* reading for the day had been *"Pay attention."* *Pay attention to what?* Eating solo she could tune into her surroundings better, that might be a start.

Jake pushed through the swinging door from the kitchen. "I thought I heard your voice. Great to see you, Olivia. What can I get you today? I'll make it myself."

"Surprise me."

He raised his brows. "Don't say I didn't warn you. Why don't you take a look around while you're waiting?"

"Is Sami or Jennifer here?"

"Sami just left, and Jennifer's home. She has daily living skills classes a couple of mornings a week. Blind Services sends someone out to help her with advanced cooking lessons and other skills. She's doing quite well. One of these days, she'll be getting her own place."

He disappeared into the kitchen, and she wandered around the café then let herself into the studio. She took extra time studying her cousin's works in progress. Adorable dog figurines covered a shelf next to a variety of hand-built pieces that were ultra-thin and smooth. Jennifer had really improved. On the far shelf sat plastic covered pieces labeled with students' names.

The cafe door chimed.

"I'm sorry. We can't accommodate lessons on those mornings."

Olivia listened to Dominic explaining Jennifer's schedule to a couple of disappointed-looking women. They bought coffees and left. She wandered back over. "Are you turning away business?"

"Yes, Jennifer's got private students and some small groups, but she has to turn away potential students. She can't be here twenty-four seven. Did you see the animal figurines she's been making?"

"Those are really cute. I love the dachshunds."

"She donates half the proceeds to South Paws Rescue." The corners of his mouth lifted, obviously proud of Jennifer. "She's come a long way." He went back to working on the computer until a group of people came through the door and the lunch rush officially started.

Jake set a delicious-looking grilled veggie and Havarti panini on the counter and she pulled out her wallet.

He waved his hand. "This one's on me. I'd sit with you, but as you can see..." He angled his head toward the line forming. "We're short today and Sami couldn't stay, so Dominic and I are covering all the bases until Lilliana can get here."

She took a seat at a booth along the wall and dug into her crunchy, gooey sandwich, studying the studio across the room as she chewed. Jennifer actually needed help, wasn't simply being nice. The studio was beautiful. She hadn't made time to stop in for a session with her cousin. Her heart dropped. Regrettably, it didn't look like she'd get the chance.

Jake was so kind to her. It'd be nice to have him in her life. But moving to Dallas made the best sense financially and career-wise. The connections she'd make working at a prestigious school were valuable. Being financially independent was huge. However imperfect, she had a plan.

~~~~~

Olivia drove toward Sacred Haven and planned her remaining days. Anna and Mark had taken it better than expected when she'd told them about the plane ticket for Monday. Last night they'd taken her to dinner at a place on the water in Sarasota to celebrate. If it didn't work out in Dallas, she'd have a home with them.

Everything was falling into place. Tonight, she'd be heading to Madison and Lexie's house for movie night with the two of them, just like old times. So why wasn't she happier? It was Trevor's fault. The way her heart leaped with excitement when he'd come over and stood next to her desk. And then her spirits had dropped when she'd spotted him through the window between classes. Next to him had stood that skinny blonde from the dining hall, Tammi, hanging on his arm and smiling like they were a couple. Feeling a little queasy, she'd snapped the blinds shut, more confirmation that heading to Texas was the right choice.

Monday afternoon she'd fly out for the interview and if everything proceeded according to plan, Mark would help her drive out later in the week. She groaned. Lydia already had a dinner party scheduled for Monday night, complete with bachelor number one of the eligible attorneys her mom had lined up.

She didn't have the right clothes for the dinner party, and Lydia would, no doubt, whisk her directly from the airport to purchase a man-hunting outfit. If there was time, she'd probably drag Olivia to the hairdresser for a more conservative style to top it off. If Olivia moved to Dallas, she'd have two jobs—teaching, and standing up to her mom. Teaching would be the easier of the two.

Marriage to a wealthy attorney made Lydia happy, but that didn't mean it was the right choice for her. Checking someone's bank account and resume wasn't at the top of her list. After all, Steele looked good on paper. Try as she may, she couldn't get her mother to see past dollar signs. They meant security. But after being burned by Steele, she preferred to earn her own money and rely on herself.

The first thing she needed to do was head to the office and give notice. She parked in front of Sacred Haven, pulled in a couple of deep, calming breaths, and drew up her courage.

Animated voices in the hall brought her to a stop. A few people were gathered around the art display she'd hung, and one of the students excitedly pointed out his artwork. A smile stretched over her face. A job at Sacred Haven Center brought its own rewards.

"Olivia, hey, Olivia." Her cousin appeared at her side. "I'm going out to ride the new horse, Sandy. Want to come?"

"Blessie, hi. That sounds like fun. But I'm teaching an art class in a few minutes."

"I'm coming to see you tomorrow. Thursday, I get to make art. Will we make more potholders? I don't like to paint. I don't want to paint, okay?"

"I have some air-dry clay you can try." Finding a workaround for someone, helping them discover they could make art despite a limitation, was turning out to be deeply rewarding.

She said goodbye to her cousin and dragged herself into the office to face Jeanette. There was no way to make everyone happy. Despite cringing at the idea of confrontation, she had to choose herself.

After she gave notice to Jeanette, the woman's mouth pressed into a thin line. "Everyone's had good things to say about you. I'm very sorry you can't stay on until—"

"Mrs. Bridges, you need to take this call. It's urgent." The secretary interrupted them.

"Make sure to stop in with your key tomorrow afternoon," Jeanette called over her shoulder, walked into her office, and shut the door.

Olivia sheepishly slunk from the office. She'd let down Jeanette and a lot of students and residents.

Her guilty feelings moved to the background when she opened the door. A large vase of red-and-yellow roses was on the desk, the intoxicating scent filling the room. Beside the vase sat a box of carrot muffins, her favorite, and a brief note signed T. *Hmm. He put some thought into this.* She opened the blind and saw Trevor talking to a small group of people near the stable. If class weren't about to start, she'd love to go thank him. Instead she laid out canvas and set out balls of clay and water.

Trevor was short on ideas for winning Olivia's heart, but food and flowers seemed like a good way to start. The gesture might say what he hadn't found the words for yesterday. Usually she arrived early, and he'd intended to see her, tell her he wanted to set things right, pick up from where they'd left off last week. To hell with his pride. If she didn't want him, she had to say it out loud.

Three notes had made it to the trash before he'd given up trying to write his feelings. He'd simply jotted a brief note to make sure she understood the food and flowers were from him, like it wouldn't be obvious. He might be going about this all wrong, but he wanted her and needed to start somewhere. The plan was to catch her this afternoon before she left, ask her to dinner, and get some alone time with her.

After meeting with a local organization that wanted its clients to get involved with the therapeutic riding, he walked into the main office. Jeanette and Mavis had some project underway, spreading files over two desks. He greeted Mavis, who was making notes on a yellow pad. Jeanette's expression brought him to a full stop. *Something's wrong.*

"What's up?"

Jeanette explained through tight lips, "I'm sorry to say we'll be looking for someone to fill that art position sooner than I hoped. Olivia's given notice. Apparently, she has something else lined up— I think she said Dallas. It was nice of her to fill in this week, anyway."

Had someone kicked him in the chest? He couldn't breathe. *Dallas? Leaving? A different position?* This was news to him.

Unable to conceal his feelings, he glanced at Mavis.

She mouthed, *"Go to her."*

He forgot why he'd come to the office and pivoted toward the door. He'd have a word with her right now.

*Damn.* Three students already sat with Olivia at the canvas covered table. Their hands were coated in slippery clay. He stepped in, making it up as he went along, and approached the table.

"Hi, Mr. Weston." Pablo held up a very lumpy coil of clay.

Robert was furiously pounding a chunk of clay, all wound up, laughing and shrieking, clearly having a ball.

"Ms. Brighton," Trevor began.

Olivia turned his way, brow furrowed, those full beautiful lips parted just a little.

This probably wasn't such a great idea.

Robert was really going at it and flung a chunk of clay to the floor next to his wheelchair. Accustomed to helping the kids, Trevor reflexively stooped down to get it, right as Olivia reached down. Her hand landed right on top of his. Their eyes met below the table.

She sucked in a breath, bit her lip. *Yep, there it was.* The look that said she wanted him as much as he wanted her. *So, what gives?*

"Thank you for the coffee and flowers," she whispered, keeping her fingertips on the back of his hand for a moment, lighting his arm on fire.

The words stopped in his throat. His body tensed and he placed the lump of clay in her hand. He wiped his damp palm on his pants and backed out of the room. "I'll talk to you later," he said hoarsely, finally figuring out this wasn't the optimal time for what he had in mind.

revor monitored the clock to get to the art room before Olivia left. Just before four o'clock he dashed through the heavy rain pounding the campus and waited in the hall. When the students left, he slipped inside her room, pulled off the dripping rain slicker, and raked a hand through his damp hair.

She continued gathering her things.

He closed the space between them. "You got a minute?"

"Sure." She pulled on a windbreaker and waved toward the flowers. "It was so—"

"I heard you gave notice, took a job in Dallas."

"Probably." She still refused to meet his eyes. "I'm flying out for the interview on Monday."

Sadness washed through him. He stepped closer, reached over, and flipped off the light switch behind her desk, leaving them in dimness, made darker by the storm outside. "That way we won't get interrupted."

She met his gaze, surprised.

He stood only inches from her. "Olivia, I don't know what happened. I thought things were good with us. I want you to know how much I've enjoyed having you here." Shit, that wasn't what he'd meant to say. The right words wouldn't come. For an intelligent man, he sure acted like an idiot around her. But what right did he have to ask her to stay?

"What?" she sputtered, blinking.

"Can I kiss you?" His pulse picked up and he searched her face. He needed to touch her. Now.

She backed up a step looking unsure but nodded just a little.

He moved in, held her cheek, and brought his lips to hers, gently. She relaxed into him and the kiss deepened. He loved the taste of her, the fragrance of her shampoo, the silky feel of her hair. He spread his hands across her back and pulled her tight. *I don't ever want to let go.* They broke apart for a moment, then kissed again. She reached up, looped his neck with her arms, melted against him. Heaven, just like Christmas Eve.

Then she pulled away.

He fought to keep his face neutral and tried to read the emotions racing across her face. She grabbed her purse and practically ran out of the room, leaving him staring at the door closing behind her. Bereft, he stood there a moment, heard the rain on the roof, the clock ticking. In that moment he realized four things. She's a woman he could love. She was leaving. He was letting it happen. If he let her go, he was a damn fool.

The windows in her car steamed up. Olivia sat in the parking lot and gulped air, attempting to still her racing heart. Rain pelted the car. Why, oh why, had she let him kiss her? And she'd returned the kiss, passionately. It was difficult enough to leave without being reminded of what might have been. She'd meant to tell Trevor herself that she was leaving, to thank him for believing in her, for helping her get the temporary position. The belief he'd shown in her had helped her move forward, bolstered her confidence. She knew she could manage a job in Dallas.

The situation was twisting her heart. A mass of conflicting feelings, that kiss hadn't cleared things up. No doubt she wanted him. But it was unclear what he wanted from her. It'd be stupid to throw away her prospects for a fling, and she didn't want a quick weekend affair. *"Pay attention."* That two-word phrase came back to her. Did it relate? What stirred inside her was deeper than attraction and scared her. But yesterday she'd seen him down by the stable with Tammi. Was that what she's supposed to pay attention to? No matter how loud her heart screamed yes, her head needed to be in charge. Tomorrow she'd come in early, meet with him very businesslike, clear the air, and thank him. They'd part on good terms. That way it wouldn't be uncomfortable when she came back for visits. After all, Blessie was quite attached to Trevor.

Oddly, thinking of how her cousin got to spend day after day in the company of Trevor caused a snake of jealousy to wind around her heart. Blessie had Trevor. Meanwhile, she was flying away from him to create a life that didn't include him. Possibly her mother would wear her down, and she'd marry some man they picked out for her. She considered the vase of flowers still sitting on her desk. Trevor didn't act like someone who had a bunch of different women. Other than Christmas, which could've been his daughter, she hadn't seen him with anyone but staff and the folks at the Center. She straightened with resolve. Before she left, she'd address the Christmas Day mix-up—and got cold hands thinking about it.

*a* night walking the grounds in the cold helped Trevor sort the mess of feelings inside him. He'd even called Mavis for advice. Since afternoon classes were cancelled for New Year's Eve, today was Olivia's last day at the Center. She was slipping through his fingers.

This was stupid—they needed to have a real talk, and soon. She was leaving Monday. The clock read only 7:00 a.m. Another sleepless night would do him in. Despite the early hour he had to drive over.

"What's up?" Mark took up the doorway and didn't invite him in.

His heart sank. The guy wasn't gonna make this easy. "I've come to talk to Olivia."

"She's not here."

Trevor glanced at the RAV in the driveway.

"I'm taking her car in for servicing. She drove Anna's car. Why do you ask?" Mark's poker face offered no comfort.

It wasn't like them to discuss his feelings, but he swallowed his pride. "Can I talk to you about Olivia?"

Mark squinted, studied him a minute, then released a snort and waved him inside.

Their short conversation went better than he expected. Olivia had gone to Jake's Café. He raced over, breaking the speed limit, and pulled in next to Anna's Toyota. He spotted her across the lot talking to Tara. It looked serious, but after a moment, they hugged, and Olivia walked his way.

Moving easily now, she was walking taller, her stride surer. In the golden rays of the rising sun, she was the most beautiful woman he'd ever seen. If he didn't do this right, he'd lose her.

Surprise registered on her face. "What are you doing here?"

He jumped out and opened the passenger side of his vehicle. "Get in, okay? I mean, will you please get in?" *Damn.* He was already screwing this up. "Would you please take a ride with me?"

One eyebrow arched, a wary look, but she climbed in. He pulled out, heading toward the key. They rode in silence for a couple of minutes. She glanced at him and sipped her coffee. He reached over and put his hand on top of hers, moving his thumb across her soft skin. She looked a little uncomfortable but didn't pull her hand away—a good sign.

"Okay if we wait to get there to talk?" He had a specific place in mind, beautiful, where he always felt peaceful, under the pines at South Cove Beach.

He held Olivia's hand and led her to the picnic table nestled among the trees. One of his favorite places, usually calming, today he buzzed with nerves. It was too early for tourists. The call of gulls and crashing waves broke the quiet. The morning sun warmed the seat of the bench. He turned sideways and straddled it so he could face her as he said his piece. If this was the last time he'd be with her, he wanted to commit it to memory. *Good God*, just being close to her squeezed his heart. He whispered her name through a dry mouth. "Olivia."

"No, no let me go first. I've been thinking."

Okay. She could go first. He'd play it cool and take the pulse on her mood. The sweet scent of whatever she wore drifted on the breeze. He resisted the urge to put his arm around her.

"Mark said you saw your daughter on Christmas."

"Uh-huh." He waited.

Her chin trembled.

*She's nervous?*

Her gaze met his.

*She has such pretty eyes.*

She looked down for a long moment, played with a pine needle, broke it to bits, then brought her face up, uncertainty flitting over her features.

His protective instincts kicked in. He wanted to ease her nerves, but he held back and listened. Mark had said she had a plane ticket. Did he even have a chance with her?

"That must've been nice, seeing her. Mark said you hadn't expected to hear from her."

Torn between confusion and the need to hold her again, he drew his brows together. "I was happy to have her surprise me on Christmas. I hope you can understand why I needed to reschedule. It's been years since I'd seen her. Is that what you want to talk about? My daughter?" *Or to say goodbye?*

She stood, pointed to the ground. "She came here—not the beach, your cottage—on Christmas afternoon?" Her gaze met his with a fiery stare, her voice strong. "If you blew me off for some other woman, I need to know. But if that was your daughter, I saw you with on Christmas..."

"Me blow *you* off?" He sprung up, walked a few steps away and shook his head, then came back and met her eyes, pulse thrumming. "I have a daughter, Cherie. She's twenty-two. She stopped in for the afternoon. That's why I tried to reschedule our trip to the beach. But for some reason, that was a problem. I tried to explain. Didn't you listen to the voicemail? You thought I had a different date? Did you...see her with me when you brought the quilt?" Anger and hurt seasoned his words. But it slowly dawned on him. *She's jealous*. He fought to keep the corners of his mouth from moving up.

"Well, at risk of sounding foolish...yes." She studied her hands. "After I dropped off the quilt, I saw you hugging a woman with long black hair. I didn't know. Then you were at the stable with Tammi a couple of days ago."

"Tammi?" He spat her name.

Olivia continued as though she'd rehearsed, then she raised her head and met his stare. "My feelings were hurt, even though that's silly, since we hardly know each other."

He took her hands. "Olivia, I'm not Steele. I don't play games, and I don't lie." He brought her hands to his lips and kissed her soft fingers. "Christmas Eve, I thought we were getting to know each other just fine."

He waited.

The wind rustled the pines above them.

Her eyes seemed to search his face, her expression soft and vulnerable.

He rubbed the back of her hands with his thumbs. "I want to know you better. I want to date, spend time together, see each other, exclusively."

She tilted her head, appeared confused or uncertain. She opened her mouth but didn't speak.

"There's nobody else..." He moved closer, brought one hand behind her head and the other around her waist and kissed her thoroughly. Then, when she wrapped her arms around his neck, he lowered his forehead to hers. "I want you, Olivia."

She dropped her arms and stepped back.

When she didn't speak, he filled the silence. "Olivia, don't go." It slipped out, just like that. Pride be damned. He'd been thinking about it all last night, had talked to Mavis, and to Mark about it this morning, had gotten his friend's blessing. He needed her here. With him. He pulled away, his pulse pounding through his entire body. "You're beautiful, Olivia, inside and out. I want you in my life. We can get to know each other better, but I've gotta tell you, I already feel like I've known you a long time."

She raised her shoulders. "I have a ticket to fly to Dallas on Monday. An interview on Tuesday."

He flinched, like he'd been slapped, but wouldn't back down. He wanted to grab her, tell her he loved her. Those three words weren't for now. They'd push her away, scare her. It was too soon. But love was what he felt. He was sure of it. "Don't go, Olivia. Stay. Give this thing a chance."

The meaning of what he was saying moved across Olivia like a tidal wave. His expression was pleading, full of promises, kindness. Slowly moving her head side to side, she processed his words. She had her tickets, had a plan. But she wanted Trevor, wanted to trust him. In a weak voice, she explained, "I was going to get a loan, get an apartment of my own, work at a private school. It's all worked out."

"Don't go. It's been a long time since I felt this way. Maybe never. Stay."

Why should she stay? What was he offering? She was drawn to him, respected him, liked him, too much maybe. She could get hurt again. *No limits.* The title of the book filtered through her mind. If she refused to take a risk, afraid she'd get hurt by Trevor, wasn't she limiting the possibility of love? If she couldn't be assertive with Anna, wasn't she putting limits on herself? Couldn't she stay and stand strong as the grown woman she was, Olivia 2.0, right here in Valencia Cove? Was it possible to reinvent yourself among people who knew you?

A long moment stretched between them. The waves beat steady on the shore. "*Pay attention.*" She met the eyes of the man studying her with an expression that seemed a lot like genuine caring. Butterflies fluttered in her chest. She opened her mouth but wasn't sure what to say.

He spoke first. "I can take a leave of absence. I have a lot of unused vacation time coming. I'll go out there, to Dallas, until you figure out what you want. I know what I want. I want you. I can... teach out there."

"What? No! You can't leave. They need you here. Blessie needs you. The residents need you."

"You mean a lot to me. I'll go if that's what it takes."

She sat down, head swimming, and her fingertips held her forehead as if to steady it. *He'd give this up, leave the center that's his life, for me?* She couldn't deny what happened when he kissed her. It was terrifying to think of trusting someone again. It'd be throwing away a shot at financial security, but she wanted to find the courage to believe him. Because being with him felt right, better than anything she could imagine finding in Texas.

She stood back up. "Okay."

"Okay?"

"Okay, I won't go. I'll give this thing a chance. You can't leave here. I won't let you. They need you here. I can stay. I can give it a chance. I... want to give it a chance."

He lifted her off the sand and spun around, elation lighting up his face. Then he pulled her in and smiled down at her. "How about we have a do-over?"

She broke into a large grin and rubbed her thumbs over his whiskery jaw before coming in for a full-on kiss. The heat radiating off him stole her breath, and she summoned the strength to pull away.

He smiled that killer smile. "I'll take that as a yes. Why don't we talk about what you want to do for a real first date?"

"I'd like that. How about after class?" Her insides lit up. She'd see him later that afternoon.

"I'll be waiting for you at the cottage."

~~~~~

*Of course he can cook.* Olivia found Trevor slicing vegetables when she arrived after classes.

He walked over, brought his lips to hers, and trailed his mouth across to her neck sending shivers through her. After a kiss on her forehead, then told her to get off her feet. "What do you like to drink? I'm making dinner."

She plopped down on his soft couch and leaned back against the colorful watermelon quilt, letting him wait on her. "Something smells good." They ate chicken and yellow rice, accompanied by beans and greens from the garden.

After dinner, he grabbed blankets and a thermos of cocoa. They drove to Crystal Sands Beach and walked a short way. He spread a blanket on the cool sand. Under the violet star-filled sky, with a bright half-moon, they talked as the waves pulsed rhythmically on the shore. The cold front had moved in, and she snuggled next to him for warmth. He spread another blanket over them, turned to her, and planted kisses across her cheek, down her neck, around her ear, sending shivers of happiness across her body. He came back to her mouth and let his passion meet hers in a deep and lingering kiss. His hands traveled down her side, across her back, pulling her closer to him. When he held her, he swallowed her up in his huge, warm embrace. His kisses were intense, passionate, better and different than she'd known with Steele.

She hated to say goodbye when she left his cottage close to midnight but drove home contented. First thing tomorrow he had the closing on the property sale. Afterward, they'd have their date, visit the botanical garden and eat lunch in the garden cafe overlooking the bay.

On the drive back to Anna's, she could think about Steele without regret. If they hadn't split up, she wouldn't have this chance with Trevor now. The disastrous end of her marriage allowed her to become more herself than she'd been in years.

Trevor said if things unfolded as planned, he had a surprise to announce at Anna and Mark's New Year's Eve party tomorrow evening. What could beat the surprise of finding love at Christmas?

"Be careful, it's hot." Anna handed Olivia the bowl of artichoke dip and allowed herself a satisfied smile. Another beautiful spread was taking shape as guests began to arrive. So far, the New Year's Eve gathering was coming off without a hitch. She shuddered, recalling Christmas Eve and that terrifying afternoon looking for Blessie.

Tonight, in contrast, happiness made all the preparations go more smoothly. Olivia had changed her plans and would stay with them until she found her own place in Valencia Cove. Not only would it be great to have her nearby, her cousin would check on Blessie when she and Mark left for their summer trip.

Aunt Lu and Uncle Ken made the trip down and would stay for the holiday weekend. She, Olivia, Tara and Lu had been bustling in the kitchen.

Lu dipped a shrimp in cocktail sauce. "I'm sorry we didn't get down sooner. Someday, we'll see more of everyone."

"Mom, we're glad Nana's okay and you and Dad are here now." Tara looked up to the ceiling. "Somehow I survived the invasion of my step kids on my own."

Lu chuckled. "It couldn't have been that bad."

Anna and Tara exchanged a meaningful look. Then Anna placed a tall yellow cake in Tara's hands. "Gosh, this smells delicious. Is it a rum cake?"

"Yes, try not to eat it all and get tipsy." Anna teased.

Tara carried it to the table and joined Jake and Lexie in the living room visiting with their Dad. Jennifer had invited Sami and her fiancée, Brice. Pastor Don and the church secretary, Susan, would be over soon. The neighbors on both sides were also coming. Matthew and Natalie wouldn't be back down, but Madison was bringing Kayden, and Trevor, due any minute, was bringing Blessie.

Mark came in the kitchen to pick up drinks and surprised Anna with a nuzzle on the neck.

She laughed. "That tickles."

In an excellent mood, having spent a good portion of the day researching RV parks for the big trip, Mark's dream was on the horizon. Olivia staying made it possible for them to get away. They'd rent an RV and leave mid-June. This year was the east coast tour. They'd start in the Jacksonville area keeping Emily and Pixie in the RV for a week. Next year, who knew? If this trip went well, she'd consider retirement, and they'd purchase an RV of their own.

The changes life was bringing made her feel like the ground was shifting beneath her, but it'd be okay. The Norman Rockwell picture of family life she held on to was falling away, leaving something more fluid in its place. New adventures were on the horizon.

Tara had given her an embroidered quote for Christmas. *"Life doesn't have to be perfect to be beautiful."* Anna loved perfect, tried creating picture-perfect experiences. But she accepted that change would be okay too. Travel meant change. Retirement meant change. Who would she be if she wasn't a teacher and the hostess extraordinaire? She was willing to find out. And if being with Trevor made Olivia happy, made her cousin want to stay in Valencia Cove, well, she could get right on board with that change.

Blessie tore into the house ahead of Trevor and headed straight for the kitchen. Olivia's heart lifted as she walked into his arms. They kissed right there in front of everyone. She rested her cheek on his chest, contentment circulating though her, scary how nice it was. Mark was watching them, the corner of his mouth turning up. If she was happy, it looked like he'd be happy for her.

Trevor pulled an envelope out of his shirt pocket and placed it in her hand.

"What's this?" She unfolded the paper to reveal Sacred Haven letterhead. The sheet was a job description for a part-time arts and crafts instructor, certified teacher preferred. There was a list of job duties. Olivia looked up. "The art position? Permanent?"

He raised his eyebrows and grinned. "You said you got your resume in order. I figured you might want to apply. Jeanette Bridges would do the hiring, and she already thinks highly you."

"I can do this." A jolt of excitement lifted her. "I loved working there this week. Do you think you could help me set up the room so I don't have to stand as much?"

"After years of adapting for people, your foot issue would be a piece of cake. If you want this job, we'll figure it out for you."

Olivia loved the sound of that. *We'll* figure it out for you. Trevor had her back. "Why, Mr. Weston, I believe I'll be talking to Jeanette first thing next week." A real teaching job, and Trevor too.

〜〜〜

Trevor strode over to Mark, who cleared off a table for the big reveal. Pulling a rubber band off the long roll of paper, he unveiled a draft of the plans for the restructured grounds. The group gathered around as he explained. Besides a rebuilt Weston Greenhouse, there was the exciting new addition of a produce stand. "I'll supervise, but we'll hire someone part-time, and residents and volunteers will mostly run it."

"Can I work in the produce stand?" asked Blessie.

"You bet." Trevor grinned at her.

"I'll volunteer there." Lexie piped up.

"Me too." Olivia grinned at Lexie.

"I wish I could." Madison shrugged. "I have sewing commissions on weekends and evenings."

Trevor pointed to the north end of the layout. "The road Seaside Development pushed for will work to our advantage. At the border of the Sacred Haven property, we'll have a ready customer base for the produce stand." His chest lifted in happiness with the new enterprise. This would generate income and give residents job skills. They'd love it.

Olivia stood beside him. Her fragrance, the nearness of her, made him want to grab her and bury his face in her neck, kissing her below the ear like he had earlier. He couldn't get enough of this woman, but he fought down the urge—after all, they were in a room full of her family. Their eyes met, and he winked. He'd mentioned the surprise when they were at lunch. This afternoon, he'd picked up the plans from the designer. It was satisfying to see it on the page.

Everyone had a question about the changes. Since Trevor's endowment was pushing the project forward, he had wide latitude over the specifics.

"Will it be called Sacred Haven Produce or Weston's Produce?" asked Anna.

"Neither." Trevor stood back, smiling at the group surrounding the table, people who'd become like family to him. He'd fallen, hard, for Olivia. There was no fighting it. She was made for him. It was the real deal, and he hoped he could convince her to make it permanent. He gave Olivia a nod then turned to Anna before announcing, "If it's all right with you, we'll call it Blessie's Produce. If it weren't for her, I wouldn't be here right now."

Blessie's face lit up, and she wrapped him in a big hug. Anna and Mark laughed. She studied the map as Mark pointed at the graphics, slowly going over it with her again.

Trevor backed away from the group, moved to Olivia, and stole a quick kiss. She gestured toward the hall. Like a couple of kids sneaking away, he followed her to the den where the tree still glowed. He circled her waist with his arm and leaned to cover her mouth with an *I want you now and forever* kiss. And then he needed another, hating to break away, having found what he'd nearly given up on. He kissed her neck and breathed in her addictive fragrance.

Memories of Christmas Eve sent waves of pleasure through him. This was where he'd been when he'd first known, had known to his bones that this was a woman he could be with. She circled his neck.

He ran his thumb over her cheek. "Olivia, I-I think the world of you." *Aw, hell, why not come out and say it?* "I love you. I know it's soon. But I'm sure."

"Me too, me too." She met his lips as he pulled her closer.

Trevor was delighted to find Jennifer had invited Sami and Brice. He and Brice talked for quite a while, and Mark got Brice on board to help coach softball when he could get away from the farm.

As midnight approached, he enjoyed a glow of contentment that had nothing to do with the twinkling lights still adorning the trees. Olivia was heading his way with two flutes of champagne. They were counting down to the new year. Usually, New Year's Eve was simply another night, but this year signaled the start of many changes. She handed him a glass. They stepped onto the patio, leaving the sliding glass door open, letting the cool breeze drift into the house. When everyone began cheering, they clinked glasses. He kissed her champagne-covered lips then rested his chin on her head. "You, beautiful woman, are better than any champagne I've ever had." His Olivia, heaven in his arms, felt like a future that promised happiness.

# AUTHOR'S NOTE

Some characters in my books are people with disabilities. My son is totally blind. Through him, and because of the years I've taught in public schools, and through the various people in my life, I've known individuals with a wide variety of disabilities. Some people prefer to be called differently abled, some prefer disabled person. No matter what words are used, the fact remains every person is an individual with strengths, weaknesses, and something unique to bring to the table of life and share with the world.

I aim to portray the people in my book with respect and dignity. And it's my intention to depict blindness and visual impairment realistically. Each person's experience and life path is unique. Even though I consult regularly with my blind son regarding my portrayal of individuals with disabilities, some people will have had a different experience than what I've shown. Such is the richness of the human experience, and no harm is ever intended.

≈≈≈

If you enjoyed this book please take the time to leave a good review so others can easily find it.

Please like and follow Juliet Brilee Romance Author on Facebook for an ongoing peek into the world of Valencia Cove, recipes, and upcoming books.

Check out my website JulietBrileeAuthor.com where you can subscribe to my blog and click the link to my sign up for my newsletter and receive a free short e-book.

Look for Book Four in the *Escape to Valencia Cove for Romance* coming in January.